This book is dedicated to anyone who ever had a crush on a celebrity and wished that they would crush on you right back! ℧

I walked through the front door, no sooner slamming it behind me before my roommate launched into a ridiculous display of begging and pleading. Not even ten steps into our Toluca Lake condo and Keri was on her knees, begging me to go out with her that night. I narrowed my eyes, staring down at her theatrics on the floor.

"But I got you a ticket and everything," she whined, batting her eyelashes up at me, as if that would work on someone as estrogen-driven as herself. "Please. It's the last show of the tour."

"I just got home and I have to work tomorrow," I told her, knowing full well my excuse wouldn't work. Keri was nothing if not persistent.

"So what? We *all* have to work tomorrow. And hello, it's Walker Rhodes. I know you like his music, so don't even pretend like you don't." When I opened my mouth to respond, she pushed harder. "And the seats are in the third row, Madison. On the floor. Sort of like I am right now." She winced and pushed herself to stand upright in all her perfect five-foot-ten-inch glory.

Keri had good reason to expect her pleas to work; she knew me so well. She and I had bonded instantly as freshmen in college when we were assigned rooms across the hall from each other. When we graduated, we went out in the world to tackle the entertainment industry together, and had been roomies and best friends ever since.

My pulse picked up with her words *third row* as I thought of how incredible every concert I'd seen from that close had been. It was one thing to be at a show in the nosebleed section, but it was almost an out-of-body experience to sit up front. Entertainers couldn't hide anything from you when you were feet away from them; you picked up the smallest details that would otherwise be missed if you were sitting anywhere else. Like the way the beads of sweat formed on their forehead first before rapidly sliding down their faces, or whether or not they were really singing versus lip-synching. You saw if their shoe came untied or if they missed a step in their perfectly choreographed routine. And don't get me started on the eye contact. Being that close to the stage gave you access to their line of vision…and you were in it.

Keri was right; I did like Walker Rhodes's music. And his face wasn't too bad either. But his reputation was a total turnoff. Not like I was planning on dating the guy, but you couldn't really think about him without having his man-whoring ways come to mind. He was in the tabloids almost daily, stumbling out of a Las Vegas club or casino with a girl on each arm, getting into fights, and spending way too much time and money there. Don't get me wrong, Vegas was all right, but anyone who loved that smoke- and debauchery-filled place as much as Walker Rhodes seemed to couldn't be good news. He was the epitome of a bad boy.

Not to mention the fact that the things I'd heard about him from some of our clients at work only further endorsed his less-than-angelic behavior. I imagined his publicist had their hands full, following behind him and cleaning up his PR messes.

"Madison, you can't make me go to this concert alone. I'll never forgive you." Keri's fake whine broke through my thoughts.

Focusing once again on her pleading expression, I laughed. "Yes, you will. And you knew damn well I'd say yes before I even walked through the door."

Her face brightened. "Actually, I just hoped you'd get home before the concert started. I never know with your hours. I was half afraid I'd have to pick you up at the office and head straight to the concert from there."

She was referring to my job at the agency. I was an assistant to one of the hottest talent agents in Hollywood, so my hours were unconventional and unpredictable, to say the least. Keri wasn't wrong to be concerned about my timing; not that her hours at the studio were any better.

I sucked in a quick breath. "I can't say no to you."

She squealed as she gripped my shoulders with her hands. "Go get ready. The car will be here in twenty minutes."

"What car?" I asked over my shoulder as I headed away from her and down the hallway of our three-bedroom apartment.

"I didn't want to drive, so I ordered a Town Car." When I shot her a knowing glance and a smirk, she admitted, "Fine, my dad's assistant ordered it, but what does it matter? That way we can drink at the show if we want to. I'm just being responsible!"

"You're wasteful with money," I said, laughing as I rushed into my room to change.

"You're wasteful with...life!" she shouted back.

I rifled through my closet and pulled out a fitted black tank top that accentuated my curves in all the right places. Then I reached for my favorite worn-in skinny jeans and slipped them on. After adding my most comfortable pair of knee-high boots, ones I knew wouldn't kill my feet after standing all night in them, my outfit for the night was complete.

I hurried into the bathroom and plugged in my heating wand, then went to work curling fat waves into my normally stick-straight blonde hair. Realizing I didn't have much time, I did a quick once-over on my face with fresh makeup. I dipped an oversized sable brush into my powder foundation before tapping it against the side of the container. Spreading a light coat over my already made-up face, I smiled at my reflection. A light dusting of gold eye shadow on my lids and some eyeliner made my brown eyes pop, followed by a fresh coat of glossy pink lipstick, and my day-to-night transformation was complete.

A glittering from the corner of the counter caught my eye and I shifted a towel to reveal my favorite headband, a gift from Keri. It was gorgeous, with two rows of Swarovski crystals set against a black elastic band.

She knew I was obsessed with headpieces. Anything that reminded me of Roman goddesses, the Roaring Twenties, or exotic kingdoms in faraway lands, and I was all over it. What can I say; I'm a romantic. She bought me the crystal one because she knew I'd never spend that kind of money on myself, claiming that my face lit up when I saw a similar one during an opening gala party we'd attended together in Beverly Hills.

I placed the headband across my head and over my newly wavy hair, which I mussed up a little so it looked fuller and the thick waves bounced in every direction.

When I headed out of the bathroom and into our living room, I saw that Keri had transformed herself into a goddess. A slinky black dress clung to every curve, and her waist-length chestnut hair fell all around her.

"Holy shit, you look gorgeous." I pursed my lips, admiring her ridiculous body. "I hope Walker doesn't see you tonight. He might not be able to sing."

She tossed her head back and laughed. "Gross. You know all those things they say about him are true, right? I mean, the tabloid stories are usually so far-fetched and out of touch with reality, but with Walker Rhodes? They're unfortunately spot-on. Such a waste."

I frowned and gave a little shudder. "I'm so glad he's not one of our clients."

"He'd be a complete pain in the ass, that's for sure. But at least he shows up for work on time and does his job. It's just all the after-hours stuff that gets him into trouble."

I nodded, agreeing with her assessment. "Hey, how'd you get the tickets anyway?"

She waggled her eyebrows playfully. "My dad. Someone at the studio gave them to him. They actually wanted him to go to the show and see how Walker performed live. I think they're going to pitch a movie with him as the lead."

Keri's dad was an executive at a movie studio. He was also her boss, since she worked for him as a production assistant. Not wanting to be accused of riding Daddy's coattails, she'd insisted on paying her dues like everyone else, but paying them under her dad's watchful eye. It garnered her respect from her coworkers that she wasn't using her daddy's name to get ahead in the business. And she worked hard, which was something we had in common.

I groaned out loud. "Not another one of those singers turned actors. Can't they just stick with one thing?" I rolled my eyes at the ceiling. "So, do you have to give a full report back to your dad?"

She nodded, waving her iPhone at me before tucking it into her purse. "Yep. I have to film parts of the show with my phone and e-mail them to him."

"You could have told me this was for work. I'll always agree to go with you to events when they're work-based."

Keri put on a serious face. "Madison, I really need you to go to Walker Rhodes's concert with me so we can stare at his beautiful face and pretend he's singing every love song to us and forget all about what a gross man-whoring pig he really is. Because it's for work." She narrowed her eyes and lowered her voice dramatically. "For work, Mads. And I need you."

I choked back a laugh as the doorbell rang, alerting us that our driver had arrived. "You're so..." I stopped myself as I searched for the right word.

"Lovable? Adorable? Amazing? I know." She shrugged her shoulders and disappeared out the front door as I followed close behind, trying not to laugh as her hair swished from side to side the same way her ass did.

I followed Keri's lead as she weaved through the slow-moving crowd. Clutching my ticket in my hand, I stopped for a moment as we passed through the double doors and entered the arena. Craning my neck to look all around, I took in the sheer number of people filing in and smiled. What an awesome feeling it must be to know that all these people were here for you.

"Madison, keep up!" Keri shouted in my direction.

"Sorry," I yelled back and rushed toward her.

"What were you doing?" Her voice was

drowned out by the hum of hundreds of people chatting around us, and I didn't respond.

"Hey, Madison! Hey, Keri! You girls look great." A tall, good-looking guy with brown hair rushed up to Keri and me. I tried not to frown as I struggled to place him, since this guy obviously knew who we were, but I would swear on my life that I didn't know him. If there was one thing I've always been incredibly crappy at, it was recognizing faces.

Having grown up in Los Angeles my entire life, I've met tons of people throughout high school, college, my internships, and now my latest job where celebrities of all types pass by my desk all day long. As a result, faces have almost become blurred to me. When you run into the people that you've watched on the television for years at places like the grocery store, the mall, and the beach, it really starts to mess with your ability to place people's faces correctly.

There have been many times I've thought that people looked familiar, but I had no idea where I knew them from. I actually walked up to a gorgeous girl at my local market one afternoon and asked her if we went to high school together because she looked so familiar. Turned out she was one of the leads in a vampire TV show that I didn't watch, but I obviously knew her face from her celebrity status. Oh, the embarrassment.

"How are you? Haven't seen you two since we graduated!" The guy beamed, his smile so wide I could see nearly every one of his teeth.

We went to college with him! The idea of narrowing down how we knew him excited me, but I still couldn't place him. "So good to see you, babe," I said as I returned his hug, and Keri stifled a laugh. She knew the second I addressed anyone as "babe" that I had no clue who they were, or where we knew them from. And most importantly, I didn't know their name, hence the "babe."

"You look fantastic, Jim," Keri responded, emphasizing his name for my reference, which made me want to both kiss her smug face, then give it a smack of a different sort. "We really have to go, though. It was great to see you." Keri tugged on my arm, and I stumbled to keep up.

Poor Jim stood there dumbfounded. "Uh, okay. We should hook up sometime! Call me!" he shouted as we walked away.

Keri waved him off with a smile as she continued to walk in the opposite direction.

"You're so bad," I called out at her back, her arm still tugging at mine.

"Me?" she shouted over her shoulder. "You're the worst! That's Jim freaking Holliday. We only partied at his frat house almost every month for like two years."

I squinted my eyes, thinking hard as flashes of college-aged Jim came flooding back. "Oh yeah! Now I remember! He had the pool table, right?"

"Yes, Madison, he had the pool table. Seriously, how do you survive without me?"

"I call a lot of people 'babe' when you're not around." I laughed as she descended the stairs, heading lower and lower through each section until she reached the arena floor. A security guard stopped us to ask for our tickets, and we handed them over.

"You're in section C, all the way to the right." He pointed at the seats lined up on the floor at the other side of the stage.

Keri thanked him as he handed back our tickets, then took my hand in hers and pulled me through the rows of folding chairs and roped-off sections.

"This is insane," I said to no one in particular as I took in the scantily clad women everywhere I looked, especially down near the stage. *Groupies.*

Ugh.

I glanced up toward the staging area and noticed a large white curtain draped from the ceiling to the stage floor. Roadies were setting up boxes, speakers, and lighting in front of the curtain in a smaller area. I assumed they were setting up for the opening act, and I found myself getting excited as we made our way closer and closer to the stage.

"Holy shit. These seats are sick," Keri said as she finally scooted into her assigned seat.

I sat down, breathless for a moment, and looked at the stage mere feet away. My heart fluttered. "These seats are amazing. Thank you for bringing me."

She bumped her shoulder into mine. "As if I'd bring anyone else."

I smiled, loving the way she always thought of me, when the sound of someone yelling my name forced me to glance around. Screaming permeated the air as onlookers pointed and flashes of light filled the otherwise dimly lit area.

"Over there." Keri pointed toward an area surrounded by security and people wearing VIP badges on lanyards around their necks. "It's Paige Lockwood. Oh Jesus, and her super-hot boyfriend, Colin McGuire. Please call them over here so I can stare at Colin's pretty face."

Paige stood arm in arm with her boyfriend, her fingers intertwined with his as she leaned into him, smiling. Her dark brown hair swept across her shoulders and down her back in sharp contrast to Colin's short sandy-blond locks. Her blue eyes sparkled, even in the dim lighting, and she looked stunning in her all-white miniskirt, long-sleeved matching sweater, and nude heels. Colin was decked out in white jeans and a black button-down shirt. They looked like they belonged on a magazine cover, which made sense considering who they were.

Paige was an actress, currently America's sweetheart and one of my boss's biggest clients. Her boyfriend, Colin, was one of the hottest singing sensations in the business, aside from Walker. Colin had been in a boy band, but had recently branched out on his own and was enjoying the huge success that had come with that decision. Where Walker rapped, crooned, and had a unique style all his own, Colin sang in typical top-forty fashion. His voice was all pop and trendy with no real soul but the public loved him, no matter how uninspired his latest hit seemed to be.

I watched as the gorgeous couple made their

way around to our seats. "Hi, Paige." I leaned in to give her a hug and an air-kiss near her cheek.

"Madison, you didn't tell me you'd be here tonight. Are you a big Walker Rhodes fan? He doesn't seem like your type," she teased, wiggling her eyebrows, and my gaze dropped to the backstage pass that hung around her neck.

"I didn't know until I got home from work and was kidnapped, forced to come here against my will, kicking and screaming the entire way." I laughed. "Paige, this is my roommate, Keri Sampson. Keri, this is Paige Lockwood." I smiled as they shook hands and exchanged pleasantries.

Keri's cheeks flushed and her voice was higher-pitched than usual as she told Paige, "I love your work. You were incredible in your last movie."

"Thank you, that's very kind of you." Paige's head tilted to the side. "Sampson, did you say? Your dad's not Howard, is it?"

"The one and only." Keri beamed with pride. She and her dad had a great relationship. He had worked long hours as he made his way up in the movie business, and was away for most of Keri's childhood, but for whatever reason, she never seemed to mind. Instead of being bitter, she was fascinated by the movie biz and wanted to be a part of his world. She started as an intern at his studio the summer she turned sixteen, refusing to take no for an answer from him.

"Please tell him I said hello. I've always wanted to work with him." Paige smiled and her trademark dimples deepened.

Colin cleared his throat and Paige sucked in a breath. "I'm so sorry. Colin, this is Madison. She's Jayson's assistant. And this is her roommate, Keri."

"It's nice to meet you," I said to Colin. He appeared less than impressed, and I felt almost bad for Paige as he fidgeted, avoiding eye contact with anyone other than her.

"Nice to meet you both," he said absently, then tugged at Paige's arm. "Babe, we should get to our seats."

Paige gave me an apologetic look before shrugging her shoulders. "It was good to see you, Madison. I have to come into the office to sign some paperwork, so I'll see you tomorrow. And Keri, it was very nice to meet you."

"Likewise," Keri said to Paige's retreating back, before turning to me with her eyes shining. "She is so flipping nice."

"I told you she was," I said, referring to all the times Keri had asked me for gossip about which celebrities were nice, and which ones were jerks. She claimed she was only being curious, but I knew it was mostly for her dad. If he expressed interest in working with a specific actor or actress, she liked to know the inside scoop on them. It was her way of watching out for him, even though he didn't need it. Howard Sampson was one scary son of a bitch when he wanted to be. And he garnered enough respect through his tenure in the industry that even drugged-up has-beens knew not to screw with him.

Ear-piercing screams filled the air. Assuming that Walker had appeared, I jerked my head toward the stage in front of me. Nothing moved, so I glanced over at the VIP area where Paige and Colin had stood a few minutes before, and noticed Quinn Johnson and Ryson Miller. This concert seemed to bring out all the local celebrities, although I wasn't surprised. This was Los Angeles, after all, and everyone who was anyone lived here. More than that, they loved being seen, so local high-profile entertainment events brought the stars out in droves.

Seeing Quinn should have surprised me even less since she was Paige's best friend. Both Quinn and her boyfriend, Ryson, were actors, although neither of them were represented by my agency.

Which was a damn shame, if you asked me, because they were both incredibly talented and we'd have been lucky to have them.

"I absolutely love Quinn and Ryson. They are the cutest couple ever, I swear. They better not ever break up. Ever." Keri rattled off her opinion at warp speed, and I half smiled as I listened to her. "Are you listening to me? If you have any control over that relationship at all, you will never let it end." She stomped her foot to emphasize her seriousness.

"How on earth would I have any control over their relationship? We don't even represent them!" I tossed my hands up in the air and shook my head at her silliness.

"I'm just saying," Keri huffed. "I think they're my most favorite young Hollywood couple. I'm invested."

"You're insane is what you are," I said with a snort.

"But I'm fun," she shot back before sticking out her tongue.

Spotlight :
a focused beam of light to highlight
a person or object onstage

After the warm-up band had finished and a brief intermission had passed, the house lights dimmed and the sound of deep drumbeats thumped, vibrating the floor and drawing excited shouts from the audience. Walker's voice boomed through the sound system, testing the mic as the white curtain dropped to the floor and disappeared altogether. The screams were deafening as his silhouetted frame appeared to rise from the floor. I found myself shouting along with everyone else without meaning to. It was hard not to get caught up in the moment, especially when you were three rows from the stage.

Slow bass beats continued as Walker sauntered from one side of the stage to the other, the rotating spotlights hitting his tanned face every so often.

When the music sped up, I recognized the tune and smiled. I thrust my fist in the air, rocking my head back and forth as he stripped off his long-sleeved jacket to reveal a sleeveless V-neck T-shirt, and a pair of well-toned, muscular arms. I screamed unabashedly along with the crowd as my gaze took in every sculpted muscle, and drank in every inked tattoo. Apparently I was more excited than I realized. He gripped the microphone with one hand, dancing to his own cadence while he sang the lyrics in his signature style.

The rest of the band remained below eye level in the stage design while Walker strutted around on an elevated platform, front and center. Usually lead singers were surrounded by a plethora of backup dancers and background vocalists, as well as several musicians. But Walker had none of those things. It was him, a microphone, and nothing else. There was pure beauty in the simplicity of the staging, and I realized I'd never seen an entertainer be more entertaining with so little before.

"Oh my God, Madison! How fucking hot is he?" Keri yelled while holding her cell phone in the air to record him.

I simply nodded in response and let a wide smile spread across my face. Was it possible that

Walker sounded better live than he did on his albums? I started to think he did. Hell, I would have believed anything in this moment. Being this close to him in his element was beyond hot. He was charming, charismatic, and sexy as hell. The way he moved with a rhythm all his own was mesmerizing. I didn't want to be charmed by him, but I was. It was like being back in junior high, a twelve-year-old girl again, smitten by every expression, every little gesture he made. My gaze followed him around the stage as he crooned into the microphone and cast meaningful glances at individuals in the crowd.

Walker sucked in a deep breath as the next song started, and he rapped as the entire arena sang along with him. I found myself drawn to the way he closed his eyes and bobbed his head, his body moving against the beat in his own rhythmic time. Not with it, necessarily. It was as if the music moved *through* him...*within* him...like every riff of the guitar, beat of the drum, and keystroke of the piano flowed beneath his skin in a way that only he could feel. He was affected by every sound that enveloped him; moved by it. And in turn, he moved me as well.

Girls screamed and he flashed a large smile,

surely knowing how that single action would elicit more ear-piercing wails. His all-white jeans and sleeveless shirt cast an even brighter glow in the spotlight as he fell to his knees, clutching the microphone tightly and singing lyrics filled with so much longing and want, it appeared as though he felt every single note in the depths of his soul.

My breathing hitched as his eyes squeezed shut and he delivered the last two lines of the song, his head bowed forward, his chin nearly touching his chest.

If I hadn't known all the crappy things about Walker, I would have thought he felt things with more intensity than other people, was a better human being. Watching him in these moments was like seeing him completely vulnerable—stripped down, raw, and completely exposed for everyone to dissect and pick apart. The emotions that radiated from him seemed so real, I was certain I could reach into the air and pull them into me.

"This is intense," I whisper-shouted toward Keri, who still happened to be recording.

"He's fucking amazing." She looked at me, her eyebrows raised. "I'm shocked he's this good," she added and I silently agreed, my head still moving slowly with the beat.

Halfway through the show, Walker Rhodes did something I'd never seen any other performer do before. A circular stage lowered from the ceiling and he walked out onto it, slowly and with purpose. He addressed the entire audience in a practiced way, talking to the crowd, mentioning girls and guys by their outfits, waving at and addressing every single fan holding a hand-drawn sign for him. The fans were overjoyed. By the time he got to the floor section where we were seated, I was ecstatic.

That had been one of the coolest things I'd ever seen an entertainer do. Watching him interact with his fans that way was both heartwarming and mind-blowing. I hated to admit I was impressed, but I was. My mind drifted as an elbow greeted one of my ribs.

"Ouch, Keri. Shit. What?" I tried to yell over the music that played in the background of Walker's salutations.

"He's staring at you," she whisper-shouted against my ear.

"What? Who is?" I said absentmindedly before

looking up toward the elevated platform. I hadn't realized my gaze had shifted away from him, I had been so lost in my own thoughts. Walker Rhodes stood directly above me, speaking into his microphone about how he "sees the girl in the black shirt with the sparkles on her head."

Instinctively, I touched my forehead and was met with the coolness of faceted crystals against my fingertips. I didn't know what to do, so I did nothing. I stared back at Walker, but I didn't smile, move, or even breathe as my heart pounded against my chest.

Then he smiled at me, and I swear part of my heart melted on the spot. I knew if I looked down at the floor, I'd see a small puddle of heart goo mocking me. For fear of looking down and having my suspicions confirmed, I simply stared into Walker's hazel eyes. At least I thought they were hazel. It was hard to tell for sure in the stadium lighting.

"Yeah you, Sparkles," he said as he pointed at me. Then he sang, "I'm looking at you. I'm talking to you. I see you," in the same melody as the background music that played. "I see you."

The Earth shifted in that moment; it must have. Because there was no other plausible explanation for why I lost my footing and almost fell straight to the floor. He broke eye contact with me and finished his endearing back-and-forth with the crowd, but my mind was reeling.

"What the fuck, Myers?" Keri shouted again, calling me by my last name.

I shrugged. It was all I could muster at the moment because I couldn't stop thinking about the way he said, "I see you." It wasn't creepy, like the way a stalker would say it, but it had the same intensity.

Wait.

Not stalker intensity. It was simply intense. I shared an intense personal moment with one of the world's biggest music gods right now. As much as I wanted to hate everything about it, I reveled in the moment. So what if I worked for a talent agency and saw celebrities every day. This was completely and utterly different.

A tap on my shoulder interrupted my reverie and I turned in that direction, only to be faced with a twenty-something-year-old girl wearing next to nothing. "Do you know him?" she asked, her clearly collagen-plumped lips puckered like she just ate something sour.

"What?" I yelled at her over the screaming

surrounding us. Taking in her tiny, barely clothed frame and the ridiculous amount of makeup painted on her face, I stopped myself from rolling my eyes.

"Do you know him? Why was he talking to you? Why does he keep staring at you?" The girl's voice was irritated and bitchy. Clearly, she hadn't dressed this way to *not* be noticed by Walker.

"I don't know him, sorry," I answered politely before turning away from her.

Still rattled by my interaction with Walker, I found myself wondering why he had focused so much of his attention on me. Breaking myself out of my own head, I glanced back toward the stage, my eyes searching for him.

Walker sat on one of the stage steps, his chin in his hand as he spoke to the screaming crowd. "I need a volunteer for this next part." His head raised slowly, his eyes scanning the crowd.

Keri jumped up and down like a crazy person, waving her arms and screaming his name. I laughed at her antics and sat perfectly still, not wanting to bring any more unwanted attention to myself.

Another tap on my shoulder caused my irritation to bubble as I turned to what was sure to be that annoying overly made-up stupid girl again.

It wasn't. I came face-to-face with a giant of a

man wearing all black and holding a walkie-talkie. Intimidated, I took a half step back and looked around for Keri.

"Come with me." His tone implied a demand, not a request, and I suddenly wondered what I'd done wrong.

Who the hell was this guy? *He's not the boss of me. He's not going to tell me to come with him and think I'll just obey.* I frowned and said quickly, "Uh. No, thanks."

He flashed his VIP backstage pass in my face as if it were the only credential he needed. "Miss. It's part of the show. Can you come with me, please? You'll be onstage with Mr. Rhodes."

Oh.

Well, shit.

I guess he could be the boss of me, after all.

I shot Keri a surprised look before I was quickly hauled off in the direction of an almost completely darkened backstage area. We walked through a black curtain before we were hit with lights and blaring music.

"I'm going to bring you onstage."

"And then what?" I asked, suddenly nervous. Not to be around Walker Rhodes, but nervous at the thought of standing in front of thousands of screaming people with cell phones ready to record my every move.

I started to tremble. Afraid my legs wouldn't hold me up any longer, I begged the security guy to help me out there. He smiled at me and gave me a little shove.

Thanks, you dick.

Next thing I knew, I was standing onstage, my face mere inches from Walker's. Walker *no-human-being-should-be-anywhere-near-this-gorgeous-in-real-life* Rhodes. His jet-black hair was clipped short against his tanned skin. The coloring only set off his light hazel eyes even more. The contrast was stunning, and triggered a tingle of awareness in me. I felt lost in that moment as I stared into his eyes, something in them calling to me. The way he stared back at me was almost expectant, like he was willing me to move, think, connect…or something.

His stare intensified and all I could think about was how I had never noticed his eyes before. Then I wondered how on earth that was even possible? Had I been blind my whole life up until this moment? The color of his eyes could stop wars from waging, or calm the roughest seas. Nothing and no one could be immune from the look in

Walker's eyes. I was suddenly hit with a sense of familiarity, but quickly tossed it aside, remembering his celebrity status. He felt familiar because he was; his face was constantly in the news and on plenty of magazine covers. Everyone knew everything about Walker Rhodes.

His mouth curved and my gaze reluctantly moved from his dreamy eyes down to a pair of deliciously full lips. My brain suddenly kicked into gear, reminding me where I currently was—onstage in front of a sold-out arena. I glanced out at the rowdy crowd as nervousness shot through me. Walker's lips moved quickly, but I couldn't hear anything because I was too busy freaking out. Although I could see Keri bouncing up and down in the audience with her cell phone in the air, which only made me freak out more.

When he leaned forward, his face almost touching mine, I could feel the electricity sparking between us. But I convinced myself it was all in my head, because really? Who wouldn't feel something between themselves and a celebrity in this moment of insanity? Walker reached out his hand and placed it under my chin to gently raise my head. And he shocked me.

Literally.

He pulled his hand away abruptly. "Sorry about that, Sparkles," he said into the microphone with a smirk before turning to address the audience. "I shocked her. We're so electric together that we spark. Just like her headband."

Then he ran his fingers gently across the crystals in a slow and deliberate motion.

What the hell is going on right now?

I forced a nervous smile as he continued talking.

"This is one of my favorite parts of the show. I love you guys so much!" The crowd roared in response as he continued speaking over them toward me. "So, Sparkles, what's your *real* name?" He pushed his microphone at my mouth.

"Madison," I said weakly before he pulled the mic back.

His eyebrows lifted. "Madison. I like it. You look like a Madison, all cute and sweet. I bet you were a cute kid."

That's a weird thing for him to say.

"Where are you from?"

I pulled my head back slightly at the question. "Here."

"Here? You're from the Staples Center?" He laughed and I smacked his shoulder.

"No. I meant here, as in LA." I shrugged.

"Well, I figured that much." He turned toward the crowd and said, "Didn't you, Los Angeles?" and the crowd screamed in response.

"So, what do you do?"

The stupid microphone appeared in my face again. "For work?" I mumbled, not really understanding why he would ask such a personal question anyway.

I felt like a complete idiot. The pit of my stomach tumbled like it was filled with rocks. Celebrities didn't normally unnerve me. I couldn't be fazed by them in my line of work, but this was something else entirely. I was coming unglued at whatever seams pretended to hold me together.

And then there was the way Walker kept looking at me. Deliberately, like he was trying to tell me something without words, but I wasn't getting the message. Maybe he was expecting me to do something, like flirt with him for the audience? All I could think about was the damn rocks in my stomach, and I felt like an idiot.

"Yeah, Sparkles, what do you do for work?" His voice boomed with confidence.

I hesitated. Should I really tell an entire arena filled with rabid fans my name and where I worked? That might not be the best idea. You never knew what people were truly capable of.

"I work at a talent agency."

There. No specifics. Los Angeles was filled with talent agents. Good luck trying to figure out which one.

"Which one?" he pressed.

Shit.

Walker flashed me a wide grin and I shook my head. "Aw, you aren't going to tell me?" He stuck out his bottom lip and pouted toward the audience. Groans and moans filled the air.

"It's not one you'd know," I lied.

"Okay, Madison, who works at a talent agency I wouldn't know, and lives in Los Angeles. This one's for you."

Walker reached his hand out for my face again and without shocking me this time, he cupped my cheek. Leaning in close, his war-stopping eyes bored into mine as he sang the lyrics to me.

I told you that I'd wait for you
But you didn't listen
So I'll fight for you
If it's what I have to do
I'll fight for you

Because there is no me
Without you
Girl, you know it's true
And now Madison from Los Angeles who works
at a talent agency
The rest of the world does too

I didn't remember that last part being in the song. And before another thought could enter my already spinning mind, his lips brushed against my cheek. Heat rose from the tips of my toes and flooded me in an instant, filling my whole body. By the time Walker pulled away, my face felt flushed and I was certain I was beet red.

He pulled the microphone away and leaned over to speak quickly into my ear. "Leave your phone number with Bob. Please?" he practically begged, his voice barely above a whisper, and the rocks in my stomach dropped to the floor and shattered into rock dust. Assuming he did this with every girl he brought onstage, I glared at him, my nervousness dissipating in a rush, only to be rapidly replaced with sharp disappointment.

"Please," he said again. "Just give it to Bob and I'll get it after the show."

Another quick kiss on the cheek, and Bob

appeared from the back to usher me from the stage. Walker whispered something to the tall man and clapped him on the shoulder, and Bob cracked a crooked smile before looking in my direction.

I was pissed. Although I wasn't entirely sure why, the moment had been cheapened by Walker. What had started as something amazing and unbelievable had turned into something typical and demeaning. All his escapades ran through my mind like a ticker tape parade. The real Walker Rhodes was a player of presidential caliber, and I knew it. I read about it online daily.

"Mr. Rhodes would like your phone number," Bob informed me before we headed out of the backstage area, as if I weren't already aware of his desires.

"I'm sure Mr. Rhodes would like a lot of things," I bit out in response.

He tugged at the black cap on his head, moving it from side to side before huffing out a long sigh. "So, you won't leave your number?"

"No." I stood firm, one hand on my hip.

"Fuck." Apparently frustrated, Bob kicked the toe of his shoe at the floor.

"He'll get over it," I huffed. "Can I go back to my seat now?"

"He's going to ask why."

I shifted my weight, annoyed at his pushiness. "Just tell him I'm not interested," I practically shouted as my emotions surged out of control. I was beyond angry, but I didn't really know why.

What the hell was my problem?

I stormed out of the backstage area and practically sprinted to my open seat where Keri was waiting, her mouth hanging open.

"What in the mother fucking fuck? Oh my God, that was so hot. You two were so hot up there. Thank God I have it all on video. You're going to shit when you see this," she squealed as she wrapped one arm around my shoulder and squeezed.

"Can't wait," I forced through a tight smile.

Two songs later, the show ended. But not before Walker said good night to the crowd and to me specifically, although he called me "Sparkles" again instead of Madison.

My ears were ringing as Keri and I were pushed along with the exiting crowd. I couldn't wait to get into the car and I hated to admit it, but booking a car service was a brilliant idea, especially after an emotional night like this.

"Tell me this isn't blissful?" Keri asked as she

scooted into the backseat and opened a waiting bottle of water.

I rested my head against the leather headrest and turned toward her. "It is."

Bad sound quality filled the back of the car as Keri scrolled through her videos and photos, stopping abruptly. Walker's muffled voice rattled me as he repeated my name.

"Madison. I like it. You look like a Madison."

"Turn that off, Keri. Please. I don't want to see it." I pressed my head into my hands and pretended to hide.

"Oh yes, you do. It's so fucking hot. It was hotter in real life, but it's still pretty hot on my phone."

I spread my fingers apart, peeking at her as she shoved her cell phone screen at me.

"Just watch it."

"I don't want to," I whined.

"And why not? Walker Rhodes brought you onstage. And he sang to you. He sang to you like he was in love with you. I've never seen anything like it." She paused to catch a breath before continuing. "Actually, he did a lot of things tonight I'd never seen before. He was pretty awesome. Didn't you think?" She turned toward me and waited for a response.

"He puts on a great show," I admitted, my tone as unenthusiastic as I could muster.

"That's it? He puts on a great show?" she mimicked before shaking her head at me. "What happened, anyway? You were having a great time at the show before you got pulled onstage. And even when you were up there, you looked like you might pass out, but you—" She snapped her fingers in the air between us. "Ugh. What's the right word? You..."

I watched as she struggled, knowing exactly what she was trying to say. I simply wanted to avoid the conversation altogether. Because if I knew Keri, and I did, she wouldn't let this go so easily.

"You know what I mean, so just answer me!" she howled, exasperated.

I turned my gaze toward the window and watched the city lights rush by in a blur. "He told me to leave my phone number with his security guard," I said softly.

"He what?" Keri squealed.

My gaze remained fixed, but I raised my voice. "He told me to leave my number and it pissed me off."

She slapped a hand on my thigh to force my attention in her direction, so I turned toward her slowly. "You didn't leave it for him, did you?" It was a sarcastic assumption more than an actual question.

I shook my head.

"Well, why the hell not?" She threw her hands up in the air as if I were the most frustrating person on the planet.

"Because I didn't want to, okay?" I shouted. "Because he probably asks every single girl he sings to every night to leave her number. I wasn't trying to be his Tuesday night fuck. And I didn't want to be one of many."

Keri sucked in a breath. "That's the real reason!" She pointed an accusatory finger at me.

"What is?" I snarled, the heat in my face rising along with my temper.

"You didn't want to be one of many. I know you, Madison Myers. You'd never date a guy who made you feel like you were replaceable. I get it."

I lowered my head. I couldn't hide anything from her; Keri knew my dating history. It wasn't like I lived like a nun, I had dated here and there, but my job was demanding and it came first.

Besides, no one…

Stop it. Don't go there. What's past is past, and you can't change it.

Defeated, I huffed out a long breath. "It was so insane up there with him at first, you know? When he touched me, sparks tore through the very fiber of my being. The fiber of my being, Keri!" I exaggerated. "It was intense. I knew it didn't mean anything, but when he asked me for my number, it made me feel cheap. Like a whore."

"Why would you be the whore? He's the whore," she snapped.

"I just felt…" I hesitated. "Cheapened. Disrespected maybe? Which doesn't make any sense, I know, because I don't even know the guy, but that's still how it felt. Like he took something magical and dipped it in shit at the end."

Keri burst out laughing. "You're fucking nuts. I love you."

"I love you too. But we are kind of avoiding the real question here," I added.

Her eyebrows pulled together. "And what question is that?"

"Why the hell did he pick me?"

> **Stalker** :
> a person who repeatedly pursues or
> harasses another in a threatening way

I arrived at work the next morning both emotionally and physically spent. Who knew that kind of excitement could take so much out of you? Tossing my purse into my desk drawer, I turned on my computer, grabbed my notepad, and poked my head into my boss's office.

"Morning, Jayson. Can I get you anything?" I stared at his messy dark hair. He already looked completely stressed out, and it wasn't even nine a.m.

Leaning forward in his expensive leather chair and staring at his computer screen, he demanded, "Get me some coffee, Madison. Also, move my two o'clock appointment with Richard to first thing tomorrow morning, and make sure I have some time scheduled before the end of the day to speak with Paige."

He pursed his lips disdainfully as he added, "I also need you to go over the finalized contracts and make sure they're correct. I sent you an e-mail with all the details. My flight to New York on Friday needs to be pushed back, and make sure they have the right meal this time."

He lifted his head and eyeballed me as he said that last part, insinuating that I was the one who had screwed up the meal, when in fact it was the airline. I learned long ago that arguing with Jayson never worked in my favor, so I kept my mouth shut and nodded my head along with his, silently taking the blame much in the same way I had when it first happened.

My boss expected perfection and didn't like to hear excuses. When something went wrong, it didn't matter how or why, but it was always my fault. I should have *seen it coming*, or *been more proactive*, or *known something like this could happen*. And when Jayson needed someone to yell at and blame, guess who won that contest every time? Me.

The thought of resigning had crossed my mind on more than one occasion, but the other agencies in the area were simply more of the same. This was an industry filled with money-driven egomaniacs. A business where personal insecurities hid under a big title and an even bigger attitude.

I scribbled furiously before meeting his bloodshot blue eyes. "Okay. Is that all?"

"For now." He waved a hand at me dismissively before looking back at his computer screen, and I rushed off to fetch his coffee.

I began working for Jayson as his assistant over two years ago, since shortly after I graduated from college. He was a big-shot talent agent, and this was one of the premiere talent agencies in Los Angeles. My plan was to work my way up to junior agent status before becoming a full-fledged agent myself. This business was complete and utter chaos...but I loved everything about it. Negotiating with producers and movie studios on behalf of your client, reading movie scripts to find the right ones, coordinating schedules and high-profile events, it was what I wanted to do.

In this business, not all actors and actresses had managers, but they all had talent agents. And I knew exactly the type I wanted to be. I planned on caring about my clients. Of course I wanted to make a decent living and I knew this career could provide just that, but I also needed to make sure that the personal relationships were what mattered the most. The talent I signed needed to trust me, knowing that I would have their best interests at heart, not just their paychecks.

I'd seen all too often how money changed people. It was like once they got a taste of the good life, it suddenly consumed them, becoming their driving force. Every aspect of their life, every minute of their time, every decision they made was devoted to doing whatever garnered them the most cash, instead of what made the most sense.

My intention was to do the exact opposite. I craved the balance that few seemed to have in this industry. I intended to work with integrity and swore to myself that if all else failed, at least I'd have that. When people thought of me, I hoped they would think of someone who had their back in the best possible way. I wanted the best of both worlds—good money and even better relationships. I would be a rarity not only in this business, but in the industry as a whole. At least, that was the plan.

Filling the large mug to the top with coffee, I hurried back into Jayson's office and placed it carefully on top of the Italian coaster he'd been given as a gift last year. Thankful I didn't spill any, I turned back toward my desk positioned right outside Jayson's door so I could begin working through my to-do list.

The red light flashed on my work phone, indicating I had a voice mail, and I absentmindedly pressed the button while simultaneously reaching for a pen and flicking my computer screen on. I was a master at multitasking.

I was furiously scribbling the details of the last message into my notebook when the next message started, but loud music and a mishmash of voices filled my ear. I squinted, glancing away from my notepad and toward the phone as I stared at it, willing it to play something intelligible in my ear. The voices grew in volume and I reached out to delete the message altogether when a suddenly clear voice stopped my hand in midair.

"Madison? God, I hope this is the right Madison. It's Walker. We met tonight. If this is the right Madison, can you please give me a call? My number is 555-8453." He paused, breathing audibly before ending the message with, "It doesn't matter what time it is. Just call me. Please."

The call disconnected and I pressed the number nine on the dial pad to save the message instead of erase it. Air whooshed from my lungs as I quickly slammed down the receiver and stared at the phone.

How did he find me? And why the hell was he looking?

Reaching for my cell phone, I typed out a quick text to Keri. I knew she'd be hard at work already, but I needed to talk to someone about this.

WALKER RHODES JUST LEFT ME A VOICE MAIL. AT MY OFFICE. WITMFF?

WITMFF stood for "what in the mother fucking fuck?" It had become one of our "things" one night after Keri had said it, and it stuck. We've been WITMFF texting ever since.

After sending the message, I turned to my computer and was scanning through the 152 e-mails waiting for me when my cell phone vibrated. I glanced at it, knowing it would be Keri calling.

"Hi," I whispered quietly into the phone. Whenever possible, I tended to avoid all personal calls while I was at the office. The truth was that I wanted to be taken seriously in this job, and so I took it seriously in return.

"Shut the fuck up!" Keri shouted. "How did he get your number? Did he leave his? Are you calling him back? What the hell, Myers?" She ranted so loudly, I had to pull the phone away from my ear.

"I have no idea how he found me," I whispered. "And no, I have no intention of calling him back."

"Why the hell not? Aren't you curious in the least about why he's stalking you?" she huffed, still yelling.

I laughed out loud and threw my hand over my mouth to quiet myself. Sucking in a quick breath, I whispered, "He's not stalking me."

"He kind of is. Shit, I have to go. We *will* be discussing this later," she informed me as she ended our call.

Placing my cell phone back on top of my desk, I focused my attention toward my computer. Scrolling through the e-mails, I quickly became annoyed at the ridiculous amount of spam that always seemed to leak through the security filters. I hated wasting even a single minute not being productive, and stupid spam always slowed me down. Once they were all deleted, I searched for the e-mails with the contract attachments from my boss. I quickly printed them out and grabbed my yellow highlighter, looking over them for any discrepancies or inaccurate information before pushing away from my desk.

Knocking softly on Jayson's door before entering, I obeyed as he held his hand in the air, indicating that I should wait while he finished typing something on his keyboard. I listened as the tapping of the keys clicked faster than any normal human being should be able to type.

"What do you need, Madison?" he asked, his attention still focused on his monitor.

"I finished looking over all the contracts and everything looks good. The addresses are correct and so are the dollar amounts." I gripped the printed papers tightly in my hand.

"Great. Send them over to the legal department and cc me on the e-mail. Did you get ahold of Paige yet? I need to see her today. Ten minutes ago, actually." He raised his head to stare at me and gave me an all-too-familiar look of disapproval.

Jayson constantly acted as if I were some inept idiot who couldn't handle the simplest of tasks, when I knew damn well that I was the best assistant he'd ever had. Everyone in the office used to tell me that. Hell, they still did.

"I'll call her right now." I forced a small smile before turning away and rolling my eyes. It was hard for me to put up with crap like this from my boss when I knew I didn't deserve it. But I figured I was still paying my dues, and one day I wouldn't be working *for* him anymore, I'd be working *with* him.

And then he couldn't treat me like shit because he wouldn't be my boss.

Sitting at my desk, I forwarded the approved e-mails to Legal before scrolling through my contacts for Paige Lockwood's cell phone number and giving her a call. Thankfully her schedule was open for the day, and she planned on making it in before lunch. At least that would make Jayson happy and maybe he'd be in a better mood.

But as for me, I now needed to reschedule his appointments to make room for Paige's impromptu visit. You'd never hear me complaining that life in the office was dull.

Paige arrived right on time and I was thankful for her considerate behavior. So many of the talent we represented didn't care about anyone else's time but their own. When they said they would be at the office before lunch, that didn't hold any weight. Talent lived by their own rules, their own schedules, and they rarely apologized to anyone. But Paige was different. She was kinder than most and never treated me as if I were beneath her.

"Hi, Madison." Her voice was pleasant and even with no makeup on, she looked beautiful. Paige was one of those naturally pretty girls. I guess you had to be in this business.

"Hi, Paige. He's waiting for you."

"What's he all wound up about? Do you know?"

I shook my head and smiled. "I have no idea. Good luck."

She took two steps away from me before stopping and turning back. "I almost forgot." A wide grin spread across her face. "Walker called me this morning. He asked me about you."

My eyes got big. "How did he know that we knew each other?"

"Well, he didn't. He called me at first to ask if I saw the part of the show last night where he brought you onstage." She angled closer to me before looking around for prying ears, and lowered her voice. "That was really hot, by the way. You two were electric up there."

My cheeks heated at the mention of our interaction. "And?" I asked, pushing her to continue.

"I told him that I saw it and asked him how he could embarrass you like that in front of all those people. He freaked out when he realized that I knew you. He wouldn't get off the phone with me until I gave him your number."

"Is that how he got it?" I asked as my jaw fell open.

"I only gave him your office number. That was okay, wasn't it? I'm sure he'll be calling you." She tightened her lips and scrunched her shoulders in an apology. "Honestly, I didn't think you'd mind."

I sighed audibly. "He's already called."

"Can't say I'm surprised. He was really determined to find you. What'd you do to him anyway?" Her face softened as she let out a sweet laugh.

"I have no idea. But you can tell him I'm not interested."

She opened her mouth to respond when Jayson yelled, interrupting our hushed whispers. "Paige? Get in here! Leave her alone, Madison, we have business to discuss. And shut the door!"

I should be used to getting blamed for everything, but it still rubbed me the wrong way. Paige mouthed "I'm sorry" as she turned away and closed the office door behind her.

I managed to leave the office before seven p.m., but not before Paige informed me that she wasn't the only person Walker had called trying to find me. By now a lot of people knew that he was looking for me, and it was only a matter of time before he showed up at the office if I kept ignoring him.

Unsure of what to do with that information, I begged Paige to tell him I wasn't interested. She tried to tell me that Walker was a good guy, but I had actually laughed in her face upon hearing those words. Paige swore it was true, but I just shook my head. With all the accounts and photos in the tabloids and on the gossip websites, there was just too much smoke for there to be no fire.

By the time I arrived home that evening, Keri was just getting out of the shower. With her long hair wrapped up in a towel, she shouted at me, "I'm dying to talk to you. Don't you dare leave the living room until I come back."

Chuckling to myself, I walked into our kitchen and grabbed a diet soda from the fridge before plopping down on our black leather couch. My stomach rumbled as I waited for Keri to come back and hound me with a million questions about Walker that I wouldn't have the answers to. But I was anxious to hear her thoughts.

"Okay, I'm here." She panted, out of breath as she sat next to me. "Ooh, give me a sip of that," she said, reaching for my soda as I reluctantly handed her the can, knowing from experience that telling her to get her own never worked. "I only want a sip, not the whole thing," she would say every time.

After swallowing a giant gulp of my soda, she folded her legs underneath her and angled her body toward me. "Did he call any more today? And are you really not going to call him back?" She cocked her head to the side, giving me a disapproving glare.

"He didn't call me again. And no, I'm not going to call him back. Why are you looking at me like you think I should? Last night before the concert you hated him too, you know?"

"But that was BOSH," she said matter-of-factly, as if I had any idea what BOSH meant. When she saw my confused expression, she said slowly, "Before. On. Stage. Happened."

I huffed out a deep breath, torn between half wanting to strangle my best friend, or end this conversation entirely by going into my bedroom and locking my door. "How does that change anything?"

"It changes everything, Madison! You didn't see what you two looked like up there. It was fucking nuts, and I'm not the only one who noticed it. Half the lot was talking about it today."

Heat spread over my face at the mere mention of people on a studio lot talking about my encounter with Walker. "They were not," I said, my voice coming out more defensive than I had intended. Finishing off the last of the soda, I placed the empty can on the coffee table at my feet.

"They were. Anyway, I think you should call him. It's not like you're dating anyone. In fact, it's been a while since you've been on any dates at all. What do you have to lose?"

"My pride? My dignity? My sterling reputation," I said with a laugh as she swatted my shoulder. Why was I so hell-bent against this anyway? Part of me couldn't remember anymore. Oh right, because Walker was the kind of guy who went out with a different girl every night. And those were not merely rumors. I'd seen the pictures. Plus, guys like him were on my Do Not Date list. At the very top.

She reached across her body for the soda and

grimaced as she realized it was already empty. With an *oomph*, she pushed off the couch and walked into the kitchen, her voice raised an octave. "Listen, Mads. I know this goes against our personal rules and stuff. You know, we don't date musicians, singers, actors, professional athletes, news anchors, yada yada, but I don't think it can hurt anything if you call this guy."

Part of the reason why Keri and I got along so well when we first met in college was that we possessed a similar work ethic. Call it occupational hazard, but both of us had insisted it wasn't in our best interest to date any potential future clientele. We both knew what we wanted to be when we grew up, unlike our other friends in college who appeared to only want to major in drinking and the inevitable post-drinking puke fest. One night in our dorm room, we made a list of everyone we refused to date based on their occupations alone. It might have been childish at the time, but we had both stuck with it and it had worked for us.

So far.

I'd seen quite a few of my coworkers fall hard for our clients, even though it went against the rules of the agency. It still happened and it never seemed to end well for my associates when the relationship eventually ended. And it always did.

I pressed my head against the back of the couch and covered my eyes with my hands. It dipped slightly as Keri sat back down with her own soda in hand. If there was a God, I was convinced in this moment that he or she existed.

"Anyway, listen to this," I began, and she leaned her body closer to mine, her eyes widening with interest as her lips puckered against the heaven-sent can. "Paige came in the office today and she told me that she's the one who gave Walker my number."

Keri fought to keep the liquid in her mouth as she choked down a swallow. "Shut the hell up! How? Why?"

"I guess he called her asking questions and she let it slip that we knew each other. He asked her for my number. She said he was really determined."

Keri tapped against her lips with one finger, obviously lost in thought. "I think you should call him. See what he wants. Maybe he'll stop calling then?"

My heart rate picked up speed. The idea of calling him made me nervous and I searched for the true reasons when it hit me. "This guy could throw me all off course. I've worked really hard at the agency and I don't want to do anything to jeopardize my career. Least of all get involved with someone like Walker and become gossip fodder. My boss would never stand for it," I admitted.

Keri's face lit up with acknowledgment and understanding. "It would be really easy to get lost in his lifestyle. But I think you're way stronger than you give yourself credit for. I've said my piece. Call him. Don't call him. I'll still love you the same."

"Thanks." I smiled, feeling slightly better about the whole bizarre situation.

> **Blackmail** :
> to force or coerce someone with
> threats of public exposure

The red light flashed on my office phone and I was half tempted to pretend it didn't exist as memories of yesterday's voice mails replayed in my mind. Reluctantly, I pressed the button and allowed the messages to filter through the air on speakerphone while I filed some of last night's paperwork into the appropriate client files at the other side of the room.

"Madison, it's Walker again. I need you to call me back. Please don't make me beg on your voice mail every night."

I raced over to the phone to pick it up and stop it from playing out loud, but it was too late.

"I mean, I will. But it's sort of embarrassing, don't you think?"

The message ended and I wished I could reach into the stupid air and grab his voice from it and stuff it back inside the phone where no one else would hear. How could I be so stupid?

Jayson's voice boomed from behind his office door. "Madison, get in here."

Shit.

He had to have heard that. Sucking in a deep breath, I opened the door and entered his lair. He motioned for me to sit down, something he rarely did, and I willed my tense body to relax.

"Why does Walker Rhodes keep calling here?" Jayson asked, his tone tinged with equal parts annoyance and intrigue.

"I'm not sure exactly," I lied.

"Do you think I'm stupid, Madison? I know he's been asking you out, asking our clients about you. Why the hell do you keep avoiding him?" He shook his head like I was a fool.

"How did you even know that?" I asked incredulously, before realizing that Paige must have said something to him.

"He's been asking around about you. Word travels quickly in this town. You, of all people, should know that." He pointed and wagged a finger in my direction.

I shook my head at his interference in my personal life, as well as the rudeness of his pointing at me, my annoyance abundantly clear. "I'm sorry. Am I in trouble? Are you mad?"

He slammed his hands against his oak desk, making yesterday's cold coffee swirl around inside his mug. "Hell yes, I'm mad. I'm mad that you keep telling him you aren't interested and that you aren't calling him back."

"Excuse me?" I choked out, clearing my throat to stop from coughing on my words, my fingers digging into the chair's spongy armrest.

"Go out with him. Go out with him and see if you can get him to sign with us. I heard he's looking for representation."

I shook my head firmly and swallowed hard before finding my voice. "No! He already has an agent. And I'm not doing that. That's ridiculous!"

Jayson grabbed a pen and began irritably clicking it against the wood, the button pressing and depressing again and again. "He has a manager, Madison, not an agent. It would be huge for us if we signed him. You will go out with him and that's final."

Excuse me?

Without thinking, I spat back, "No, I will not."

He couldn't force me to go out with him.

Could he?

This was ridiculous.

Jayson's face was devoid of emotion as his features hardened into stone, and I felt all the color drain from my own. "You will too. If you want to keep this job."

"Are you threatening me?" I asked, my voice shaking.

"Call it workplace advancement. You go out with him, get him to sign with us, and I'll promote you to junior agent a year before your time."

"I don't want the promotion that way." My stomach churned at the nasty deal that was being presented to me. I'd never dealt with this sort of harassment in the workplace before. Yes, I'd seen people do horrible things to other people, but I'd never been a part of it.

Drawing in a gulp of air, I searched my mind frantically for an out, then leaped upon one last chance. "I thought we weren't allowed to date our clients. That it's frowned upon, maybe a conflict of interest? I could get fired for dating him."

"I thought you liked this job," Jayson sputtered as he threw the pen to his desk.

"I love this job," I admitted honestly.

His eyes narrowed. "Then I'd suggest you do whatever it takes to keep it. I could make it very difficult for you to get another one in this industry."

My eyes started to fill and I forced the tears not to fall, refusing to cry in front of my asshole boss. I wouldn't give him the satisfaction of knowing he beat me. He had me by the lady balls, and he knew it.

"Fine. I'll call him."

"I knew you'd come to your senses. Now go." He waved me away with a flick of his wrist and looked back down at his laptop.

My legs felt like shaky rods of lead as I walked out of Jayson's office. Part of me was incredibly pissed off by the threat he'd made, while the other part was just plain defeated. I felt cornered and I panicked, so I gave in when I should have fought back. Silently, I berated myself for being so weak.

I almost turned around and marched right back into Jayson's office, but suddenly realized that if I didn't call Walker, I could lose it all. Jayson wasn't bluffing, and I had worked too damn hard to walk away from this job willingly. Plus, guys like my boss were a dime a dozen in this screwed-up industry. I needed to learn how to deal with personalities like his, not run away from them.

Listening to my voice mails, I typed Walker's number into my cell phone and sent Jayson an instant message saying that I would be right back. I couldn't make this call in the office where there were so many people around. The conversation about to happen was too juicy for even the best-intentioned people to resist listening in on. The only way to eliminate the curiosity was to make sure they never knew it even happened.

As I walked out the building's glass doors into the sunshine, a gust of wind sent my hair flying all around me and I struggled to push it back into place with my free hand. Dropping my oversized sunglasses in front of my eyes, I carefully walked down the steps toward the busy sidewalk. Cars whizzed and swooshed past me, creating way too much background noise, and I imagined myself plugging my ear with one finger while yelling "Huh? What did you say?" over and over again into my cell phone. Glancing in both directions, I made up my mind and headed down the side street, away from the congestion.

When the passing traffic lessened and I could actually hear myself think, I punched SEND and started chewing nervously on my thumb as the phone rang. With shaky legs, I hopped up to sit on the decorative concrete wall that circled my office building.

"Hello?" Walker's groggy voice filtered into my ears and I instantly flashed back to being onstage with him. And his incredible eyes.

Good Lord.

"Hello?" he asked again.

I cleared my throat before responding. "Walker? It's Madison."

What the hell was I supposed to say to him? What if he hadn't even planned on asking me out? This had been a stupid idea.

"Madison!" His voice instantly cleared and he suddenly sounded chipper. "I'm so glad you called. Paige said she didn't think you would. What changed your mind?"

"Uh, I don't know?" I smacked my head with the palm of my hand.

He laughed, and it made me smile. "Okay, Sparkles. I'll cut to the chase. Will you please let me take you to dinner tonight?"

"Tonight?" I almost choked, the balmy Southern California air suddenly feeling thick and suffocating.

"Yeah. Tonight. Why waste time? I want to see you."

Still unable to wrap my head around the fact that Walker Rhodes was interested in me, I stuttered, "Why? You don't even know me."

The line was silent and I actually pulled the phone away from my ear to make sure our call hadn't disconnected. When I realized it hadn't, I pressed it back against my head and waited for his response.

"I'd really like to," he finally said. "Get to know you, that is. Let me take you to dinner. I can pick you up, or meet you there. Whatever makes you the most comfortable."

Frustrated that I was being forced to do this to keep my job, I said tightly, "I'll meet you there. I'd rather take my own car. What time and where?"

"Eight o'clock at Vine's."

I clenched my teeth, knowing how fancy a restaurant Vine's was. It catered to the celebrities and always made their clientele comfortable, but it was ridiculously expensive. Dealing with the rich and famous all day long definitely helped fuel my need for normalcy at night. A place like Vine's was somewhere I'd never normally frequent, not that I hadn't eaten there before. I had. Many times. But truth be told, I always hated it. I wasn't into the whole "see and be seen" lifestyle, and it made me uncomfortable.

Glancing down at my work attire, I was

thankful I hadn't worn jeans that day. My knee-length leopard print skirt that I'd paired with a long-sleeved black silk blouse would definitely work for dinner. Not to mention the killer black heels I sported. I wouldn't have to go home and change if I needed to work late; I could just head straight there from the office.

"Madison? You know where it is, right? The one in the city, not the one in Santa Monica."

I resigned myself to a night of uncomfortable opulence. "I know where it is. I'll see you there." Ending the call before he could say anything more, I immediately regretted that I hadn't called him from my work phone. Now Walker Rhodes had my cell phone number.

Damn it.

I'd have to deal with that later.

Carefully, I hopped off the wall and thought about looking up the Vine's website when I got back to my desk. It had been over a year since I'd last been there and I liked to be prepared, so I would check out their dinner menu online and have my order carefully picked out before I arrived. At least the fake dinner date would go quicker that way. No pesky details to hem and haw over.

I typed out a text message to Keri as I walked

toward my building's entrance.

GOT BLACKMAILED INTO GOING OUT WITH WALKER TONIGHT. JAYSON SAID IF I DIDN'T GO OUT WITH HIM HE'D FIRE ME. GOING TO VINE'S TONIGHT AT 8. KILL ME NOW.

My phone beeped with a text response as I entered the elevator and pressed the button for the eighth floor.

KILL YOU? I'LL KILL JAYSON. YOU KNOW THAT'S NOT LEGAL. IF HE FIRES YOU, I'LL HELP YOU SUE THE LIVING SHIT OUT OF HIM AND THEN YOU CAN RUN THAT COMPANY.

A quiet giggle escaped as I read her words and I knew she was right. What Jayson was doing wasn't legal. But I felt trapped, and I knew how things in this industry worked. Shit like this happened all the time, and if you filed a lawsuit, the whole town would know about it and you'd be blacklisted before you updated your résumé. This was a who-you-know industry in a big who-you-know town. I planned to keep my mouth shut and do what I was told, no matter how much I hated it.

I popped my head around Jayson's door and knocked quietly before announcing, "I have dinner with Walker tonight. Just thought you'd want to know."

A sinister smile spread across his face, a face I could no longer look at without wanting to beat into a pulp. "Great. Where are you going and when? Make sure you talk business."

I sighed. "Vine's at eight. I can't promise that he'll sign with us. I have no control over what this guy does with his life. But I'll try, okay? That's the best I can do."

Jayson gave me a smarmy smirk and said, "I'm sure you can do better than that," before turning back to his work.

> **Bread** :
> a food whose main ingredient is wheat or
> meal, usually leavened and then baked

I handed the valet the keys to my Jetta and silently
hoped that Walker would already be waiting inside.
The last thing I wanted was to be here before him,
which was why I'd purposely arrived fifteen
minutes late. If the swarm of paparazzi outside the
brick building were any indication, Walker was
already here.

One of the guys lugging a camera leaped
toward me as I adjusted my skirt and blouse, but
another camera-wielding life-ruiner touched his
shoulder and said, "She's no one," as I moved to
enter the restaurant. Nothing made you feel better
than hearing a low-life paparazzi jerk-off call you a
"no one."

After weaving through the maze of outdoor
seating, I followed the short pathway to the front

doors. As I stepped inside, the hostess looked up from her podium with a fake, tight-lipped smile.

"Good evening. Do you have a reservation?" Written all over her Botox-injected face was the fact that she hoped I didn't.

"I'm meeting Walker Rhodes for dinner. Do you know if he's here already?"

Her expression soured as she took me in from head to toe before announcing, "Ah, yes, he is. You're late. Right this way."

I followed behind her perfectly sculpted ass and fought the urge to trip her just so I could watch her fall. All this hostility toward me lately was making me violent. I needed a drink. Heads turned and eyes watched me, tracing my path, obviously curious if I was the one meeting Walker in the back. He might have been in a more secluded section of the restaurant, but everyone still knew he was here. I suddenly wished I was better at faking it.

When the hostess waved her hand toward the booth where Walker was waiting, I flashed a closed-mouth smile and muttered thanks in my snarkiest voice.

"Problem already?" Walker joked and I noticed how relaxed he looked, leaning casually into the back of the booth with a beer in hand. The long sleeves of his unbuttoned flannel shirt covered up his tattoos and his well-sculpted arms.

Pity.

"She's sort of a bitch. Sorry I'm late. Traffic," I lied.

"No problem, I planned on waiting all night if I had to." His hazel eyes met mine and I gave him a quick grin as I felt myself blush at his words.

"Come, sit." He patted the seat cushion next to him in the semicircular booth and I scooted into it, leaving enough space for a person or two to fit between us. The configuration was awkward, and I wished we were sitting across from each other like normal people.

He leaned over and gave me a lopsided grin that made my heart flutter. "You can move closer. I don't bite."

I closed my eyes a second to keep from rolling them, then said, "I'm good. Plus, I don't even know you. You might bite."

Okay, I might have flirted back. I wanted to hate him or be annoyed by him, but it was really hard when he was this close. His stupid good looks disarmed me, even though I wasn't normally the type to fall at a celebrity's feet. I couldn't in my line of work. But Walker was nothing if not charming, without even trying. It seemed like he was simply made that way. If you took one smidgeon of allure, mixed it with two dashes of handsome, tossed in a devilish grin and eyes that could stop world wars, you'd have Walker Rhodes. And *that* irritated me, which in turn reminded me that I was here against my will.

Thankful for the prompt service from our waitress, I turned my attention in her direction and away from Walker's innate animal magnetism.

Rahr.

"Good evening, my name's Rachel. Can I start you off with something to drink?"

"Yes!" I responded a little too enthusiastically and Walker chuckled into his fist. I shot him a glare before asking, "May I please get a whiskey sour?"

"Absolutely," she said with a smile. "I'll be right back."

Rachel was a petite brunette with a flawless complexion and stunning makeup skills. She definitely fit the bill of the stereotypical stunning actress/waitress, if that was indeed what she was. She was also clearly used to waiting on celebrities, but even I could tell that Walker's presence had her rattled. I had to commend her on her ability to remain professional, when I would bet a hundred bucks she'd be willing to service him *under* the table as well as over it. For a second I almost wished she would. At least that way I could end this charade.

"Whiskey, huh? Didn't take you for a whiskey girl, Madison. Rough day?" His finger idly followed along the rim of his beer glass in a circular motion.

"You could say that." I really hadn't intended to be so cold, but I didn't understand what he wanted with me in the first place. Sure, we shared a moment onstage, but big deal. Walker shared that kind of moment with a different girl every night. And honestly, this all felt like a colossal waste of my time.

"Are you irritated with me? Did I do something wrong? I mean, how is it possible I've screwed this date up already?" His head tilted and a smirk appeared.

Squeezing my eyes shut for a second, I sucked in a quick breath and decided to be brutally honest with him. "I'm sorry. I guess I just don't understand what we're doing here."

Walker lifted his arm in a sweep to indicate the room. "I thought we were having dinner."

I narrowed my gaze at him. "I know that. But

why? What did I possibly do to intrigue you this much?"

"You ask a lot of questions." He licked his lips before taking a sip of his beer. After placing it back on the table he leaned toward me, his eyes locked onto mine. "Why don't you just try to enjoy yourself instead of trying to figure me out?"

A ragged heartbeat or two crept by before I shrugged my shoulders, clearly admitting defeat. He wasn't going to let me out of this easily. "Fine." My tone came out sounding bored and uninterested.

"Fine," he mimicked with a good-natured grin as the waitress placed my drink in front of me and I hastily reached for it.

Taking a sip, I closed my eyes briefly as the liquid coated my insides in warmth. "Mmm. I needed that."

Glancing over at Walker's ridiculously handsome face, I placed the glass against my lips and tilted my head all the way back, draining the contents as the ice in the glass splashed against my upper lip. Grabbing the cloth napkin in my lap, I dabbed it against the wet parts of my face.

"Whoa. Slow down, Sparkles."

"You just can't help yourself, can you?" I shot him a look of irritation and he laughed.

"What? The nickname? I like it. Plus it's a hell of a lot funnier when you look like molten lava could shoot from your ears at any moment. Definitely no sparkle there."

A million comebacks fired into my brain at once, but I chose not to engage the beast and instead lifted my empty glass meaningfully toward the oncoming waitress. She nodded before turning around to return to the bar.

Not a fan of drunk driving, I immediately started second-guessing my additional drink request. Sucking my bottom lip between my teeth, I bit down nervously as I weighed my options in my head. I could always take a cab home if I needed to. It would be a colossal pain in the ass, especially since most places didn't allow you to leave your car parked in their lot overnight, but it was a much safer option than the alternative. I'd also bet that Walker would be all too willing to give me a ride home. Biting down a bit too hard at that thought, I gasped before releasing my lip and noticed that his eyes were trained directly on my mouth.

Our waitress appeared again, breaking his laser-beam focus, and I smiled before stirring the amber-colored liquid instead of drinking it. My head already felt heavy and the last thing I needed was to start seeing two Walkers instead of one. One was already more than I could handle.

"Do you two know what you'd like to order, or do you still need a few minutes?"

I remained silent, refusing to admit that I'd studied the menu before I came, and waited for Walker to answer first.

He shook his head. "I still need a couple minutes."

"No problem," she said with a kind smile before heading away with an extra swish in her backside.

"Do you know what you're getting?" he asked.

I reached for my menu, which had remained unopened since I arrived. "Uh, nope. I'd better figure it out."

"Pretty much everything they serve here is amazing, so you can't go wrong with whatever you order."

"Good to know." I pretended to study the menu, taking my time reading each item slowly in order to avoid Walker's mesmerizing eyes. I berated myself for acting like an idiot, making this situation far more complicated than it needed to be. Slamming my menu shut, I leaned back into the booth and looked right through him. Or at least I attempted to.

"You know what you're getting?"

"Yep," I answered confidently. "You?"

"I always get the same thing," he confessed with a slight shrug.

"Shut up! You do not. Then how do you know if everything's good or not?" I teased, my head swimming from a toxic mixture of alcohol and charm.

"Everything here *is* good. Trust me."

"Trust you? Not a chance." I gaped, shocked that I'd actually voiced those thoughts out loud, and slapped a hand across my mouth after the words escaped.

Walker didn't even flinch. Instead, he raised his eyebrows and asked sarcastically, "Let me guess? You believe everything you read in the tabloids?"

Embarrassed, I glanced around the room, determined to look everywhere except his eyes. "Do I look like someone who believes everything she reads in the tabloids?"

"Five minutes ago I wouldn't have thought so. But now, I'm not so sure." He took a swig of his beer and swallowed deeply.

That was a definite insult.

He just insulted me.

Jerk.

I reached for my drink, but decided not to even

go there until I had some food in my stomach, and grabbed my untouched water instead. After drinking half the glass, I countered, "Well, just for the record and not that it's any of your business, but I'm not the kind of girl who believes everything she reads. But I do tend to believe the things I see. Over and over"—I paused for effect—"and over and over and over again." I smirked.

He leaned in so close, I could smell him. His personal scent mixed with the beer he'd been drinking, and it swirled together in a blissful union before traveling up my senses and imprinting itself on me. "You shouldn't believe everything you *see* either."

I guffawed. "Typical!"

He leaned back, his expression incredulous. "What?"

"That's just such a typical response. God, you're such a guy."

His eyes twinkled as he tipped up his lips into a smirk. "Glad you noticed."

And there was the cockiness I'd heard so much about. I'd be damned if it wasn't a complete and utter turn-on.

Our waitress returned, our conversation pausing as she took our order. I asked for a basket of their signature homemade bread while we waited for our main course, certain I'd be more than tipsy soon if I didn't eat something.

Tipsy led to bad choices.

Bad choices led to Walker Rhodes.

I needed bread. Stat.

Still nursing the same beer he'd had since I arrived, Walker took another small sip before wiping at his lips with the back of his hand. His flannel sleeve slid up a bit with the movement and I caught a glimpse of one of his tattoos. I wasn't normally a big fan of tattoos, but had to admit that they suited him.

A basket of warm bread appeared in front of me and I dug into it like a starving animal, grabbing a huge chunk from the partially sliced loaf. When I looked up at Walker, he was laughing.

"Oh my gosh," I said through a mouthful of bread. "Don't laugh at me. I'm starving."

"I'm not laughing at you. You're fucking adorable," he said so nonchalantly that I almost choked. "And you eat carbs. It's refreshing."

"Your charms won't work on me, so just save your breath," I warned as I tried to convince myself those lies were true.

"Is that a fact?"

"Mm-hmm," I mumbled, my mouth filled with warm, carby goodness. It was so damned tasty I was tempted to stand up in the middle of the restaurant and remind all the female patrons what they were missing. *"Eat the bread! It's delicious! Screw your diet!"* I wanted to scream. What had happened to our generation anyway? Denying ourselves good food was just plain senseless. Oh well, I thought, more for me. And my ass.

"You keep making faces like that and I might have my way with you right here in this booth," Walker whispered, his breath warm in my ear.

When had he moved that close?

I snorted. "In your dreams, pretty boy."

"Pretty boy?" he choked out, hitting his chest with his palm.

I turned my head toward him and offered a tight-lipped smile. "Well, you are sort of pretty."

And he was. Like many celebrities, he had a gorgeous tan, although up close his didn't look artificial. And those eyes. I needed to stop looking at them. The longer I stared, the more they attempted to render me useless and stupid. He wanted me to be stupid.

"Thanks, I think." He glanced away, shaking his head and moving his lips, but no sound came out. "No. Fuck that. I don't want to be pretty. Pretty's for chicks. I'm not a chick."

"Trust me, I know you're not a chick," I said as I reached across him for another piece of bread, my hand brushing against his, causing a familiar spark from the concert to come to life and rush through me. Startled, I pulled back quickly, empty-handed.

"That's good." He sighed. "Didn't want to have to show you just how much of a man I really am."

"I've already read about it in all the tabloids anyway," I said with a snicker.

Walker shot me a sidelong glance and said jokingly, "You're a pain in my ass. Remind me why I wanted to see you again?"

I shrugged. "Hell if I know! That's what I keep asking you."

"You really don't remember, do you?" His lips puckered and his eyes looked wistful as confusion clouded my brain.

"Remember what?"

He sucked in a breath before waving me off. "Nothing. Never mind."

"Are you talking about the concert? Of course I remember the concert."

He tapped his fingers against the table, and looked away. "Yeah. The concert."

"You're weird." I stuffed another bite of bread into my mouth, already feeling much more in control of my senses and less affected by the alcohol from earlier. I finished off the rest of my water just to be safe, and left my second whiskey sour untouched.

"Yeah? Well, you're the one at dinner with me."

"Not by choice." The words tumbled from my lips before I could stop them.

Shit.

The spoon he'd been fiddling with dropped to the tabletop and clanged against it, the sound cutting through my eardrums. "Wait. What did you just say?" Walker's tone tightened instantly, no longer amused or flirtatious.

Anxious energy swirled in the pit of my belly as I thought about not answering at all. Shoot. I needed to fix this, but how?

"Madison. You said you weren't here by choice. What does that mean?"

I met his eyes and answered honestly. "My boss made me come tonight."

"He *what*? Why the fuck would he do that?"

The anger and hurt in his voice stirred up my sympathies, and I fought off the urge to wrap my arms around him and tell him I didn't mean it.

"Because," I said lamely, pausing as I tried to think up a good lie. I went with the easiest response. "I don't know."

He narrowed his eyes and pointed a finger at me. "Don't lie to me. Don't fucking lie to me, Madison."

It was a demeaning and infuriating thing, to be pointed at. "Don't point at me!" I snapped as he looked down at his finger before pulling it back, his face still hard.

I'd always prided myself on my personal integrity, but this was a new low for me. In this moment I was no better than my boss, or any of the other assholes in the entertainment industry who did shady things to get ahead.

"He wants you to sign with him, okay? He heard you were looking for an agent and he wants it to be him." I looked away from him, instead focusing on the patterns in the grain of the wood tabletop.

"Is that why you're here?" he bit out, his tone sounding angry and confused, and maybe a little bit betrayed.

"Yes," I admitted with a huff, my involvement in this situation making me feel like a total dirtbag.

"Did you come here tonight for any other reason?"

"No," I answered, my gaze still locked on the table.

"Tell me something then, *Madison*." He practically sneered my name, as if saying it caused a bad taste to form in his mouth. I didn't have to see him to imagine the disgusted look that must have been on his face. "If your boss hadn't made you come here tonight, would you have come on your own?"

I didn't know if it was because his pointing at me had pissed me off, or if the way he practically spat my name did, but my answer was brutal in its simplicity. "No."

"Leave."

My gaze raised slowly from the table to meet his face, his expression anything but disgusted and angry like I had imagined. He honestly looked hurt, which confused my heart and made it flip-flop inside my chest. This entire day had been filled with nothing but drama, and I hated drama. Which was ironic considering the business I was in.

"I said leave! Get out of here!" he shouted, and everyone in the restaurant turned to face our table. "And you can let your boss know that I wouldn't sign with his company if it was the last agency on Earth."

You could have heard a breath being sucked in, if anyone was breathing at all anymore, which I was certain they weren't. Mortified, I grabbed my black clutch and scooted out of the booth, practically sprinting for the exit as I prayed I wouldn't stumble in my three-inch heels. Heat flared in my entire body as dozens of eyes burned holes in the back of my head.

Only once I burst out of the restaurant doors and the cool evening air hit my face did I suck in a freeing breath.

I had a reprieve.

Little did I know how short that reprieve would prove to be.

Paparazzi :
freelance photographers who pursue
celebrities and take candid photographs

Cameras flashed all around me as the paparazzi screamed my name and asked where Walker was. The fact that they knew my name eluded me in that instant as I struggled to see my own hand in front of my face, the bright flashes blinding me with each burst of unnatural light. I practically threw the valet my ticket, partly because I couldn't see him, but also because I was so desperate to be anywhere but there.

How mortifying had this night been? *Ugh.* And all because my boss had threatened my job.

"Madison! Madison, wait!" Walker called out as he burst through the restaurant doors behind me. I turned to face him, but it was pointless. I couldn't see a damn thing.

The paparazzi went nuts, shouting both Walker's name and mine as flashes surrounded us.

"Just leave me alone, Walker," I spat. "I'm sure you can find someone in there to take home tonight. Try the hostess. She looks easy."

The men with the cameras all oohed and aahed at my comment before firing off their own questions and comments as Walker gritted his teeth.

"Aw, don't be mad at him, honey."

"Walker, what did you do to her?"

"Why are you fighting?"

"What did he do to you, sweet Madison, honey?"

"Madison Myers, look this way!"

"Did you meet her at your agent's office?"

That particular question almost stopped me in my tracks. How did they possibly know exactly who I was and where I worked?

"She does work for your agent, right?"

"How long have you two been dating under the radar?"

"Does everyone in the office hate you, Madison?"

"I bet they're all jealous!"

When the valet pulled my car up in front of the painted curb, I rushed toward the driver's side as cameras continued to flash in my face. "Seriously?" I cried out. "I can't see. Please." I was practically begging, desperate to leave. This night couldn't possibly get any worse.

"Leave her alone. Let her get in her fucking car!" Walker's voice boomed at the group of celebrity stalkers, and the ones nearest me took a step back.

I slid into the driver's seat and slammed the door just as my passenger door swung open and someone jumped inside. Glancing over, I saw Walker straightening his shirt as I tugged my seat belt around me.

"What the hell? Get out of my car!" I shouted.

"No. I'm not going anywhere," he said stubbornly. "Now get us out of here and away from these cameras so I can talk to you."

"I don't want to talk to you." I closed my eyes, willing his body to magically eject from my car.

"Why are you so goddamned difficult? I'm not the incredible asshole you seem to think I am. Just drive, please, so we can talk this out." The sound of his seat belt clicking let me know he had no intention of leaving.

Opening my eyes, I looked directly into his and decided to stop fighting the internal battle that raged within me. "Fine. But where am I supposed to go?"

"We can go to your place."

I breathed out a half laugh. "Are you high? I'm not bringing all this chaos to my door. Hurry, Walker. Tell me where to go."

"My house is gated. They already know where I live. We can go there," he offered with a small smile and I agreed, even though the last thing I wanted was to be alone with Walker Rhodes...in his house.

I think.

"Fine," I said again, realizing that I'd said that word more times tonight than I'd ever said in my life.

"It's in Malibu, though. I hope that's okay."

Malibu. Shit, that's far.

"Wait? Are you okay to drive?" He placed his hand on my thigh and gave me a gentle squeeze as I lurched the car forward. When I tightened my leg muscle and looked down at his hand, he quickly removed it.

"I feel okay. I must have eaten a whole loaf of bread in there. If I feel the slightest bit off, I promise I'll pull over and we can call a cab."

"Sorry," he said and stared out the passenger

window, although I wasn't entirely sure what he was apologizing for.

"Malibu's kinda far, you know." I had no intention of driving forty minutes to Malibu through the dark and winding roads of the Pacific Coast Highway, only to have to drive back home later. I glanced in the rearview mirror, taking note of cars racing to keep pace with us.

He glanced back at me. "How far is your place?"

I shook my head wildly. "It's close. But I'm not taking them to my condo. I don't have privacy gates. They'll surround the place."

He nodded, tossing a glance over his shoulder and out my rear window. "They will. Shit."

"There's gotta be a way we can lose them," I said as I pounded on my steering wheel in frustration.

The fact that Walker was in my car and that he'd left his at the restaurant hit me at that exact moment like a ton of bricks. I was suddenly worried that I'd have to drive back to the restaurant so he could pick up his car at some point. The last thing I wanted was to act like his personal driver. Hell, I didn't even want him in my car right now.

"How are you getting your car?" I asked. "You

left it at the restaurant."

He shrugged. "Doesn't matter. We need to figure out how to lose these guys."

"You know that never works," I said with a sigh. Our clients had recounted horror stories about how the paparazzi followed them relentlessly, almost causing accidents just to get a single picture that might or might not get sold. Their behavior was not only ridiculous, it was dangerous.

"Think, Walker!" I demanded. "Come on, you deal with this every day. I don't. You have to be somewhat prepared."

"They already know where I live," he said with a shrug, "so I don't try to lose them anymore. There's no point. They usually follow me home and sit across the street until I go somewhere else."

"We could go to my office!" I glanced over at him, thrilled that I'd thought of it. "It has pass-only underground parking. They won't be able to get in."

"No." His voice was adamant. "I don't want to go anywhere near your office, Madison."

How could I have already forgotten what I admitted to him at dinner? Was it still considered dinner if you never actually got to the main course?

"Screw it," I said before suddenly making the

next right.

"What are you doing?"

"I'm going home. It's not like they can get inside my building, and my condo doesn't face the street."

His hand landed on my thigh again. I tensed immediately but he didn't move it. "Are you sure?"

I sighed. "Let's just go before I change my mind."

Ten minutes later, I pulled my car into my designated parking space, then quickly shut off the engine and clicked off the lights. We both jumped out in a rush and headed toward the locked building entrance. Cars screeched to a stop behind mine, paparazzi jumping from their cars and snapping pictures in a frenzy as the tinted glass doors closed and locked behind us.

Feeling unable to breathe until I was safely away from prying eyes, I punched the elevator button repeatedly and waited, shifting from one foot to the other. I peeked over at Walker, worried he'd be annoyed it was taking so long. "The stairs are all the way on the opposite side of the building and we're on the fourth floor. This is usually quicker. Sorry."

"Don't worry about me. I'm fine. Are you

okay?" He shielded my body with his, making sure only his back was visible. It felt strangely intimate to be protected by him. And I liked it. But I didn't want to.

The elevator made a sound that was a mixture of a ding and a broken doorbell before the door shuddered open. He hesitated and I smiled. "It's just old. Come on."

He stepped inside and the doors closed behind us, leaving us truly alone for the first time since we'd met. His body inched closer to mine, closing the space between us, and I struggled to catch my breath at his nearness.

"What are you—"

My question was cut off by the feel of his lips pressed against mine. Before I could get lost in his lips, I shoved at his body, breaking our contact. "What the hell?"

He rested his palms on the wall behind me, trapping me as his body pressed against mine. "I need to kiss you. Not want. Need. And I'm going to do it again, right now. So don't stop me."

His lips were back on mine and I lost the will to fight. All reason escaped me as I instinctively wrapped my arms around his neck and pulled him tightly against me. An overwhelming feeling of familiarity swept through my body and soul. The taste of beer still on his breath only served to fuel my arousal as his tongue teased my lips, begging for entry. I parted my mouth, allowing him in, and moaned as his tongue met mine for the first time.

Walker bent his body, his hands reaching down to cup my ass in my skirt, and I fought against the urge to hop into his arms and wrap my legs around his waist. I suddenly wished I were wearing jeans. His hands moved from my ass to my hair, but his mouth never left mine. His actions were deliberate, every flick of his tongue against mine a calculated act. And I loved every second of it.

No, no, no. I can't do this with him.

I pushed him away as visions of his past conquests came trotting through my mind. "Stop," I managed to say as the elevator also came to an abrupt halt.

"Madison." He reached for my hand and gripped it tight. "Don't be mad."

"God, Walker. We don't even know each other. You can't just do whatever you want with me." I attempted to formulate a reasonable argument without admitting just how much I liked the way he did whatever he wanted with me.

I didn't want to be that girl, though. You know,

the kind who fell for a celebrity simply because he was too hot to resist in real life. I was slowly becoming the type of girl I not only didn't respect, but didn't like. Walker Rhodes was ruining my life.

Turning left after I exited the elevator, I walked past three dark blue doors before reaching mine. I tried the handle before reaching for my house key. It was unlocked and I led him into the entryway.

Keri shouted from somewhere in the condo, "That better be you, Mads! I want to hear every fucking detail about your night with the hot—" She rounded the corner in her pajamas and her eyes went wide as she took in Walker's tall frame standing in our living room.

"Shit." Keri normally had a good poker face in uncomfortable social situations, but this one must have been too much for her because her face turned bright red. I couldn't wait to tease her about it later. "Um, hi." She extended her hand, practically drooling at the sight of him. "I'm Keri, Madison's roommate."

Walker shook her hand politely before releasing it. "I'm Walker. It's nice to meet you."

She gave me the stink-eye before leaning over and hissing in my ear, "Thanks for the warning. I could have changed, you know."

"Sorry," I whispered back.

She then stepped back and crossed her arms over her chest. "What the hell are you two doing here?"

Walker shrugged and answered for both of us. "It's a long story."

"Well, I have all kinds of time," Keri offered and I shot her a death glare. "Um, just kidding. You two kids probably want to have some time alone, so I'll be in my room." She turned to walk away, then looked back. "But Walker, will you hate me if I go all fan girl on you right now and ask you to take a picture with me?"

I groaned. "Keri!"

Walker visibly relaxed and laughed. "It's fine."

Keri practically shoved her phone at me and insisted I only take it from the "tits up" since she wasn't properly dressed. After approving the picture, she tensed and made an odd face. "Can I ask you one more thing?" she said, directing her question at Walker.

"Uh-huh," he responded, before giving me a quick glance.

"Will you please sign something for me?" She slapped her palms together so it looked like she was praying. "I'm sorry, Mads."

"Where's my roommate and when is she coming back?" I teased.

"I know! I swear I never act like this. And I meet celebrities all the time." She slapped a palm against her forehead. "I'm such an idiot. Okay, I'm leaving you two alone. Promise." And with that, she disappeared down the hall and closed her door.

"She's funny," Walker said with a smile once she was out of sight.

"I've literally never, and I mean *ever*, seen her act like that."

"You're going to give her shit for it, aren't you?"

I let out a big grin. "Until the day I die."

After the whole elevator incident, I struggled with
where to have this conversation Walker so
desperately insisted we have. If I allowed him into
my bedroom, I was convinced that absolutely no
talking would occur. Unless you considered body
parts being inserted into other body parts talking.

Tonight had already gotten more out of hand
than I ever intended, so my bedroom was definitely
out. And that left the living room. Yes. The living
room would be a safe zone. Keri could walk out at
any moment, and the couch was large enough to put
ten people between us.

"Can I get you anything to drink? Or eat? Shit,
Walker, you must be hungry. Do you want me to
make us something?" I offered, feeling only half
bad that we left the restaurant before eating dinner.

My feelings wouldn't allow me to take full blame for that debacle since he was the one who insisted I leave. I wanted to be angry at him for that, but I couldn't be.

"Do you cook?" His voice raised an octave, the idea clearly exciting to him.

I chuckled. "I'm not sure you'd call what I do cooking, but I survive on it."

"How about you leave the cooking to the pros, and just grab us some snacks?" he suggested, and I wanted to kiss him for being so brilliant.

"Sounds great. Do you want a water, a soda, or beer?"

"Water sounds perfect, thanks."

I went into the kitchen and grabbed two bottles of water, a few pieces of fruit, chips, crackers, cheese, and napkins, then walked carefully into the living room, trying to juggle everything in my arms.

Walker jumped up when he saw me. "Let me help." He reached for the box of crackers and pulled it from my arms, causing the entire pile to crash to the floor.

When I laughed at the mess, his cheeks flushed. "I'm sorry." He swooped down to grab everything before I could. "Where should I put it all?" His glance darted between the sofa and the cluttered coffee table.

Pushing all the knickknacks on the table to one corner, I motioned for him to place it on the empty space. He dropped everything into a heap and I busily set them up, arranging the snacks in an orderly manner. Or at least a manner that made sense to me.

Walker reached for one of the bottles of water before sitting down on the couch, one foot tapping restlessly. He patted the cushion next to him and I kicked off my heels, then sat down and maneuvered myself a little farther away from him than necessary. His face scrunched up as his eyes narrowed. "Seriously?"

"You're the one who said we needed to talk, so I'm maintaining a safe distance from you and your magical eyes."

"My wh–what?" A laugh escaped from his lips, and I decided that those were magic too.

"Nothing." I rubbed my eyes with my hand, trying to break away from every part of him that called to me. "You said you wanted to talk?"

"I did. I mean, I do." He rolled his bottled water between his palms, staring at it for a moment before saying, "First of all, I want to apologize for losing it in the restaurant tonight. I'm so sorry about that, Madison."

When I raised my hand to stop him, he waved me off. "I shouldn't have acted that way, but I just got so pissed off by what you said." His head lowered like he was too ashamed to look at me. "It's just that I didn't want you to be there because you had to. I wanted you to *want* to be there."

Pulling in a deep breath, I waited to see if he would continue. When he didn't, I jumped in. "I understand why you got upset. It was a shit move on my part and it was rude. If the roles were reversed, I would have been upset too."

His eyebrows drew together and he shook his head. "But I shouldn't have yelled at you like that. There's no excuse. My mom woulda kicked my ass."

"Look at me, Walker," I pleaded. "I'm the one who feels like a jerk. I should be apologizing to you. So, I'm sorry."

He turned his gaze to the floor. "Can I ask you something?"

"Anything," I said, hoping I wouldn't regret being so generous.

"Why didn't you want to go out with me?"

I started to spout off, *Why the hell did you want*

to go out with me? but stopped myself and calmly said, "Because you didn't seem like my type."

"What's your type?" His eyes bored into mine as he waited for my answer.

"Not the guy in the tabloids with a different girl each night."

His eyes grew wide. "So you just believed all of it? You don't normally believe the things you read, but with me all bets are off? I'm just such a scumbag that of course whatever they print must be true. Right?"

"God, Walker, no," I lied, although his words actually reflected how I felt. Or used to feel. "I mean, I don't know. I had no reason to believe otherwise. Should I have?"

The outraged look on his face confused me as I wondered what the point could be to all of this.

"You didn't stop to think for one second that there might be more to my story than what meets the eye?" he demanded, and my insides suddenly filled with guilt. Why the hell was I feeling guilty when Walker was the man-whore in this situation, not me?

"Why would I?" I shot back. "It seemed so obvious the type of guy you were. Not like it's surprising in this town. Why would I question it?" I didn't want to hurt his feelings, but I didn't want to lie either.

He twisted the cap from his water and tossed the cap on the coffee table, then took a small sip. "I guess you're right. It probably does look really bad. My publicist keeps telling me to tone it down, but I've never seen anything wrong with it."

I sighed, my hopes for Walker being decent plummeting more with each second that passed. "Most guys like sleeping around. I can see that you wouldn't be the exception to that rule."

Walker choked in mid-swallow and reached for a napkin. "You think I'm sleeping with all those girls they take my picture with?"

"Aren't you?"

He coughed and pounded at his chest with his fist before taking another gulp of water to clear his throat. "No. Listen, Madison, what do you know about me?" He leaned his body forward to close the gap between us and I defensively leaned away, my skin pressing back against the cool leather of my couch.

"Not much." I shrugged. "I know that you've been singing most of your life and that you grew up in Malibu."

"Stop. That part." He looked meaningfully into

my eyes.

"The you-grew-up-in-Malibu part?" I scrunched my face, not understanding what he was getting at.

"I'm from here. I've lived here my whole life. I went to school and played music at the same time. Those girls that I'm always photographed with..." He blew out a breath and reached across the space between us to touch my cheek, and my eyes closed for a second at the warmth of his skin. "Those girls are my friends. They always have been and they keep me out of trouble. As long as I'm with them, I'm not going home with some groupie who wants to use me so they can sell a story. So yeah, you might see pictures of me leaving with a new girl every night, but I've known that person pretty much my whole life. I'm not some crazy player who has one-night stands anymore. Jesus, do you even listen to the lyrics of my songs?"

He sounded offended as my mind searched to not only recall some of Walker's songs, but the lyrics as well. In this moment all I could think about was his fingers on my skin and that kiss in the elevator. But he was right. His music was romantic, the lyrics filled with sweet words and deep emotions. They were songs about lost loves, albeit sometimes sung in a rap god sort of way.

"So you've never slept around? Nothing they say about you is true?"

His gaze flicked away as he lowered his head and massaged the back of his neck with his fingers. "To be honest, after my mom died, I went a little off the rails."

"I'm so sorry."

The months after his mom passed away filtered into my memory. Gossip-laden headlines sprang to my mind as I recalled that period in Walker's life. That was when he started making the news daily in a negative manner.

"She was really sick," he said in a low voice, then looked up at me. "You remember?"

My eyebrows knitted together as I sat there perplexed. "Remember? What do you mean?"

Walker stared at me for a moment, and when I said nothing more, he said, "Sorry, I just figured you'd remember from the press or the news or something. Anyway, when she finally died, I was happy she wasn't in pain anymore, but I'd also lost my best friend. She was my biggest fan, you know? So I drank too much, screwed too many girls, and almost blew it all. That's when my friends stepped in. They told me I was out of control and that I was going to ruin everything I'd worked for my whole life. And they said my mom wouldn't be happy. That practically fucking killed me."

He grimaced before looking straight at me. "Don't hate me for this."

Touched by how vulnerable he was making himself, I said, "I won't."

"Promise," he insisted.

I smacked him on the shoulder. "I can't promise."

"Then I'm not telling you."

I groaned. "Okay, okay. I promise."

"You promise what?" he prompted.

"I promise I won't hate you."

"My friends pretty much staged an intervention, but they called it a whore-vention." He tried to smile but couldn't, and I giggled at the name. "They made me promise that if I was going out, at least one of them had to be with me. And I didn't have to stop drinking, but I had to stop giving all my money to strippers and the blackjack table, and I had to stop fighting strangers and stop sleeping with random girls. That's basically it."

He winced and asked tentatively, "So, do you hate me?"

I had already assumed that Walker was as typical as they came. After all, I'd been familiar with his antics before going out with him this evening. If I felt any emotion at all at this point, it was understanding. "No, I'm shocked actually. I can't believe no one's ever put it together that the girls are the same."

His face relaxed and he nodded. "I know, right? I never go to a club alone and I always leave with the same friends I came with. It's just that no one sees that part. They take their pictures, they angle them a certain way, edit them, crop them, do whatever they want and say whatever they want, and people believe them."

The lack of bitterness or anger in his tone surprised me. He sounded completely at peace with it all.

"I wouldn't be able to stand that," I confessed.

"Which part?"

"The part where people thought things about me that weren't true. I'd go nuts," I said with a small laugh.

He reached out his hand and took mine in his. "You would go nuts trying to change everyone's opinion of you. That in itself is a full-time job. There are some things you just have to let go of, and that's one of them."

"It doesn't bother you?"

He shrugged. "Depends on what they say."

Glancing up at the clock on my wall, I noted how late it was. "I don't mean to be rude, but I really need to get to bed. I have to work in the morning."

Walker glanced toward the clock as well, then frowned. "We haven't talked about your work yet."

"I really don't want to. Not tonight. Can I tell you about it some other time?" Considering how my emotions had been so up and down from the events of the entire day and night, it was a wonder I hadn't crashed already.

He cocked his head to one side. "You really weren't going to go out with me?"

"I wasn't even going to call you back," I deadpanned.

"Ouch." Pushing himself off the couch, he reached for my hands and pulled me to my feet. His lean frame towered over me, especially now that I was barefoot. Taking a step toward me, he tugged my body hard against his as sexual awareness zapped through me. When he kissed the top of my head, his breath warmed my hair.

I may never wash my hair again.

Oh my God, how fan girl is that?

His fingers splayed wide as his hands pressed

against my lower back. Each touch from him sent electricity racing through my veins.

Relaxing, I wrapped my arms around him and hugged him back with just as much intensity. I pulled him against me, holding him tight, savoring the contact between us. It was amazing how things had changed in the course of a few hours.

Walker stiffened, then pulled back slightly, his grip on me loosening. "Shit. I don't have my car."

My head dipped at the realization. "That's right. Do you need me to drive you back to the restaurant to get it?"

Please say no.

"Nah. I'll call a cab."

"You sure?"

"I'm sure." His fingertips gingerly guided my chin upward to face him. "Unless you want me to stay here with you tonight?"

Adrenaline kicked into high gear as my knees practically buckled with want. Thank God I was wrapped around him for support. Before I could formulate an answer that made a lick of sense, his soft, full lips were back on mine, attacking me pleasurably. He nipped my bottom lip with his teeth, tugging it into his mouth as he sucked on it. I melted into his movements, his actions, his very being.

The thought that I should stop this briefly entered my mind, before exiting stage left just as quickly. I'd spent so much time judging this man without knowing him, assuming everything printed about him was true. But after everything he'd confessed to me tonight, I liked the Walker Rhodes who currently stood in my living room, making love to my lips and teasing me with his tongue.

I wanted more of him. My body ached for all of him. But not tonight. Reluctantly I moved my hands from around his neck to the front of his chest and pushed away lightly, breaking our connection. "You need to go," I said playfully, giving him a rueful grin. "Or I'll never let you."

"That's not a good way to get me to leave." He kissed the top of my head once more, then reached into his pocket to pull out his cell phone, pulling me close again as his arms wrapped back around me and his fingers punched at the screen behind me.

"Do you think the paparazzi are still here?" I asked.

He blew out a breath and shoved his phone in his pocket. "I forgot about them. They might be. Hopefully they got bored and left. Not like there's much to report from this location, and getting pictures of me by myself are nowhere near as fun for them as getting pictures of me with random girls."

"Go then. You sure you're fine calling a cab?"

"Already called."

"When?" I pulled back from him to meet his eyes, wondering just when the hell he called a cab because I'd never heard a thing.

"I have an app. It lets them know I need a pickup and from where, and then I get a text when they're outside. It comes in handy. I sort of want to marry this app."

I smirked and said, "This sounds serious. I wouldn't want to come between you two."

"Too late." A smile crept over Walker's face as he leaned down to press his lips to mine one last time. "I plan on doing this a lot, so you'd better get used to it." His tongue swept across my lower lip before sneaking into my mouth and teasing mine.

My mouth moved with his, never breaking contact as he threaded his hand through my hair, then cupped my head and tugged me closer. I pulled at his neck, wanting him closer, as if him pressed completely against me wasn't close enough. He groaned and the vibration sent messages of lust straight between my thighs. His erection pushed against my body and I rubbed myself against it. I wanted to rip off all his clothes and have my way with him on the carpet in my living room. Classy, I know, but I was more turned on at this point than I could ever remember being. It had clearly been a while for one of us.

Cupping my ass, he squeezed, the action followed by more moans escaping from that perfect mouth of his, before he moved away and I instantly hated his absence. His lips moved across my jaw line before traveling down my neck, and I tilted my head back, luxuriating in the pleasure he gave me. I wanted him to take all of me, to lick every square inch of my body. If he asked me again if he could stay, I'd scream out the word yes and then spend the rest of the night doing things with him that people only wrote about. We were both adults, for God's sake. We could do it on the first non-date if we wanted.

Right?

Oh God, I'm a total floozy.

When a chirp sounded loudly from Walker's pocket and he reluctantly moved his lips from my neck, I wanted to cry out from the sudden loss, to yell at him to put his lips right back where they were and not to ever stop. I focused on breathing, calming down the ache between my thighs, and gathering my wits.

Never in my wildest dreams did I think that this was how my night with Walker was going to end.

"My cab's here." He looked at his phone with regret, both of us so filled with desire I swear it circled in the air above us, begging us not to stop.

I swallowed, unable to speak since my breathing was still erratic and my mind was mush.

"I'll call you tomorrow." He smirked. "And don't think I won't. This right here," he waggled his finger between our bodies, "isn't over."

One last soft kiss on the lips and he headed out the front door. I leaned against it and sank to the floor. That was without doubt one of the hottest nights of my life.

So far.

Integrity :
incorruptibility; honest; a strict
adherence to a code of ethics or morals

The following morning I woke up, not quite sure which parts I remembered about last night were reality and which were a dream, especially after the rather sexually explicit one I'd just been having. I rolled my neck from side to side before stretching my arms toward my ceiling and rolling out of bed.

Last night I'd all but forgotten about the fact that I wanted to know why Walker was so hell-bent on seeing me and going out with me. Every doubt, question, and concern in the world completely disappeared the moment his lips had touched mine.

Stupid magical lips.

But as I brushed my teeth, replaying the events of yesterday and his confessions from last night, I couldn't have cared less about the whys of it all. Gratitude was my overwhelming emotion, as I was so damned thankful that my boss coerced me into going out with Walker.

Stupid, beautiful, wonderful, magical lips. When will we meet again?

I must be ill.

Feeling my head for a fever and confirming the lack thereof, I started getting ready for work. Keri was already gone, so I knew I'd be dealing with a barrage of questions from her later. The thought made me laugh out loud.

Once I'd dressed in faded blue jeans with a sand-colored sweater and matching ankle platform boots, I pulled my hair back into a messy bun. Gold clutch in hand, I headed out of my building, completely oblivious to my surroundings as I walked absentmindedly toward my designated parking space. The sound of clicking and questions being shouted at me almost made me drop my purse as my eyes shot up and looked straight into multiple camera lenses.

I was not prepared to be met with the paparazzi. Walker had sent me a text that the parking lot was clear when he left last night, but they must have come back early this morning. So I was caught off guard as men carrying cameras closed in all around me, shouting questions.

"Madison, are you dating Walker?"

"Did he spend the night?"

"Is he still in there?"

"Are you pregnant?"

What? I stopped walking and turned to the gaggle of sleazy men. "Are you kidding? Jesus. I'm not pregnant and I need to get to work. Please move so I don't run you over."

Hopping into my car, I put it in reverse and backed out slowly, the cameras pressing against my car windows, the sound of clicks echoing all around me before they pulled back and disappeared as quickly as they had appeared.

Glancing into my rearview mirror, I noticed the line of cars that followed me. They already knew where I worked, and it wasn't like they could get into the building. Why they continued to follow me, I had no idea.

Maybe they think I'm going to see Walker?

I weaved carefully through traffic, my motions deliberate and slow, hoping the paps would catch on that I was actually headed to work and leave me alone. It wasn't until I made the last left turn onto Wilshire Boulevard and clicked on my turn signal that they sped off, obviously content knowing my destination.

The elevator mirror revealed the stress from the morning's activities as I noticed pieces of my updo falling all around my face. Instead of fixing it, I decided to leave it alone, my hair the least of my worries. I passed Jayson's office on the way to my desk, the familiar red light flashing at me mercilessly. The sight now brought an awkward smile to my face.

"Madison, come in here, please." Jayson's voice pleasantly boomed from behind his office wall. At least he sounded happy.

Holding my breath, I walked into his brightly lit office.

"Come sit. Here." He pushed an unopened bottle of water my way as I warily sat down. "So, how was your date with Walker? Did you two have a nice time?"

Jayson was suddenly attentive, his tone agreeable and overly sweet, which caused my stomach to churn at its fakeness. I almost asked him to stop, the disgust roaring through me too much to take this early in the morning. Plus, he was trying to ruin my magical evening, cheapening it, and I hated the very idea.

"Is he going to sign with us?" Jayson beamed at me, a smarmy smile transforming his aged and sun-beaten face.

Uncertain how to break the news to him that Walker wouldn't be signing with him, I decided to cut to the chase and just spit it out. It would inevitably have to come out anyway, and it would be in my best interest to leave out the part where I spilled the beans to Walker about the real reason I agreed to go out with him. There was no need to get into any more trouble over this, which I was certain I would be. Getting into trouble, that is.

"He's not signing with us, Jayson. I'm really sorry."

But I wasn't.

His face immediately turned an unnatural shade of crimson as his hands balled into fists on top of his desk. He looked like a child who had just lost his favorite toy. "And why the hell not? You obviously fucked this up for us, Madison."

"Me?" I coughed out, my voice a mixture of disbelief and irritation. "I only went out with him because you threatened my job! I tried to talk to him about signing here, but he doesn't want an agent right now." I lied through gritted teeth and prayed he wouldn't see through my bullshit.

"Oh! Well, that's a different story altogether now, isn't it?" His face started to return to its normal coloring. "Why didn't you just say that in the first place?"

"Sorry." I wasn't certain which parts I was apologizing for, or why I apologized at all, but it seemed like the right thing to do at the time. What was it about bosses and their ability to manipulate you into thinking they owned you? Why did we tend to let them get away with things we'd never let *normal* people in our lives get away with?

"So, you'll be seeing him again then, I assume? Make sure you give me all the details so I can set up the paps."

The room spun around me as my vision blurred. "*You* called them?" The realization of how all the paparazzi knew my name and where I worked slammed into my consciousness like a freight train.

"Of course I called them," he said, looking rather proud of himself. "You have any idea the amount of publicity you've given me? I got at least a dozen voice mails and a hundred e-mails as a result of it. Other agencies have been trying to land Walker for years."

"The paparazzi are relentless, Jayson. They followed me to my house last night! They were there when I opened the door this morning!" I gasped, the air closing in around me as I tried to make sense of it all.

"You can deal with it. You're a big girl. I want you to keep dating Walker until he makes up his mind on an agency." His bloodshot eyes settled on mine. "Not that anyone else would touch him. They assume he's already made his choice. And when he does, it better be this one. Don't make me look like a fool."

I sat back in the chair, bristling. "Uh, no. I won't do that."

"Excuse me?"

"I said no." My defensive instincts kicked in. I refused to let this slimeball I called a boss do this to me again. "I'm not your pawn, Jayson, or your whore. I'm your assistant. And what you're asking me to do is beyond unethical."

His fists slammed down hard on top of his desk, causing my unopened bottle of water to tumble over and roll to the floor. "Unethical?" He let out a sinister laugh. "You have no idea just how *unethical* I can be," he threatened.

"I won't do it." I shoved out of the chair and stood stiffly in front of his desk, trembling with anger and the injustice of it all.

"But you will," he said smugly. "You love this job. You're good at it too, and I know how badly you want to keep it. So, you'll go out with Walker until he signs with us. After that, I don't give a fuck what you do with him." His attention abruptly shifted from me back down to his keyboard. Apparently our conversation had ended.

My throat constricted again and I wished I'd had some of that water. "No," I croaked out.

"*No*?" His voice sounded shocked as his gaze slid menacingly back up to meet mine.

"No. I won't go out with him. I won't force him to sign with us and you can't make me. This is illegal, Jayson. This is bullshit!" I spat at him, completely disgusted.

"I dare you to find anyone in this office who would agree with you," he said coldly. "If you ever want to work in this town again, you should choose your next words carefully." He suddenly pointed a ballpoint pen right at me, reminding me of the way Walker had pointed at me last night, and I lost it.

Completely fucking lost it.

"I've worked for you for over two years," I said tightly, "and I've never once complained. I took all your bullshit craziness and handled it like a champ because I wanted to get ahead in this industry. I wanted to be an agent here. But if this is how you do business, I want no part of it. You disgust me.

This whole place disgusts me." I waved my arm out toward the door, indicating everyone who sat outside of it.

I referred to Jayson's bosses. As much as I'd like to think that they were clueless in how he handled his business, I knew better. All anyone cared about was the bottom line. Their lives revolved around money, and I wanted mine to be more than that.

"If you think this industry is filled with rainbows and sunshine, sweetheart, you've got another think coming." Tiny balls of spit formed in the corners of his mouth as he continued shouting. "It's a dog-eat-dog world out there, and if you don't eat the fucking dog, you get eaten! You have no idea what it takes to get ahead. And even if you did, you don't have the balls to do it. You'll never make it as an agent. You're too soft."

"Fuck you," I shot back. "I'd rather not be an agent if it means I have to treat people the way you do. I value the basic human decency you lost a long time ago, if you ever had it to begin with. I feel sorry for you, and I never want to be like you."

"You never could," he said with a sneer. "You're weak and pathetic."

My heart pounded as I gripped the back of the

chair for support and leaned the upper half of my body toward Jayson's desk. "And you're an asshole who doesn't care about anyone but himself! I hope all your clients see you for who you are and dump your sorry ass."

He barked out a mean laugh. "I make them way too much money, they'd never leave me."

"You mean, they make *you* money," I shouted incredulously, my temper rising to an all-out boil. "Not the other way around. They don't work for you, Jayson. You. Work. For. Them. No wonder you're so screwed up."

He snorted. "You're so naive. You've just signed your own death warrant in this business, sweetheart."

"We'll see about that," I shot back with confidence, but wondered how much weight he truly held outside these office doors. "And don't call me sweetheart."

"Get the fuck out of my office," he shouted, spraying spittle all over his desk.

"Gladly," I said coldly. "I quit."

I turned around as quickly as my shaking legs would move and slammed his office door with all my strength. Something in his office rattled and crashed to the floor as I stalked to my desk, and I allowed myself a satisfied smile.

The office was eerily silent. All my coworkers were standing up in their cubicles, peeking over the partial walls with wide eyes focused on me.

I grabbed my clutch and the few personal items I kept here as well, and walked hastily toward the elevator. A few hesitant claps broke out in my wake, but the rest stayed quiet. My face burned as I wondered what they were thinking.

In the parking garage, anger seared through my veins, charring everything in its wake. Even the tears that threatened to fall failed to form, choked out by my anger and the adrenaline that still pumped through me. Reaching for my cell phone, I dialed Walker's number. It didn't even register at the time to think it odd that he was the first person I wanted to call.

When he answered the phone by crooning my nickname, Sparkles, the tears sprang free. I couldn't speak; I just sobbed. I needed to get it together, but I had no idea that hearing his voice would affect me like that.

"Madison, I was kidding," he said quickly. "I won't call you that anymore. Are you there?"

When I sniffled, he breathed out a sigh into the receiver. "Are you crying? What happened?

Madison?"

"I just quit my job," I managed to get out before repeatedly sucking in jagged breaths.

"You quit?" He paused for a moment, and I could hear him breathing. "What happened?"

"C–can you come over?"

He paused, but it was too long a pause. I'd made a mistake in calling him. I was just about to tell him to forget it and tell him I was sorry for bothering him when he asked, "Can you meet me out here instead?"

I nodded.

"Madison?" He repeated my name, obviously unable to see me nodding through the phone.

I nodded my head again like an idiot. "Yeah. I can meet you there. Where?"

"The Ripcurl Café in Malibu. You know the place?"

My heart stopped beating and I nearly dropped the phone in my lap. Yeah, I knew the place. I hadn't thought about that restaurant in years, and now that he was suggesting it, I wanted to throw up. I couldn't go back there. I'd vowed never to step foot in that place again. And I hadn't. Not since I was a teenager.

"Can we go somewhere else?" I said, my voice shaking. "I'd really rather not go there."

He's going to think I'm crazy.

"It's my favorite spot. You don't hate it, do you? You can't hate it."

"I don't hate it," I murmured, my mind sorting through the memories I'd locked away tightly all those years ago. Every single one of them flooded over me and I started to hyperventilate. Concentrating on my erratic breathing, I willed myself to calm down. It was only a restaurant and it had been a lifetime ago. Surely I could go eat there with my new friend, and not completely lose my shit over it?

I hoped.

"Madison?" Walker's voice broke through my semi freak-out, instantly calming me.

"I'm here." I took a few deep breaths, trying to calm down. Just because I'd had my heart ripped out at that café as a teenager didn't mean that I needed to act like one now.

Grow up. You need to move on.

"Can we go there? I'd really like to take you there." His voice was overly chipper and I suddenly wanted to smack him for it.

"Fine."

Walker sighed. "I have a feeling that when you say 'fine' you're just giving in, but that doesn't mean you're happy about it. I promise you'll be happy about this. Meet me there in an hour."

"Fine," I said again, and hung up.

> **Memories :**
> recollections; past events, facts, or
> impressions that have been recalled

The moment I pulled my car onto Pacific Coast
Highway, my chest tightened. Being in Malibu
hadn't made me feel like this in years. It wasn't the
town bringing back all the memories, it was the
venue.

Turning right into the café's gravel lot, my
heartbeat quickened. As I pulled into a parking
space, I thought about turning right back around
and leaving. I'd simply tell Walker that I couldn't
do it. We'd have to meet somewhere else. Shaking
my head as I took deep breaths to calm myself, a
quick rap on my window caused me to jump and
my breath to catch.

Walker's hazel eyes greeted me through the
glass, their familiar color imprinting on me again. I
narrowed my eyes as I examined the flecks of green

and brown in his, their soulful depths virtually calling me home. Or maybe just to the bedroom.

"You all right?"

I collected my thoughts at the sound of his voice and pressed the button to roll down my window. "Sorry. Give me a second." I breathed deeply again, reminding myself that I could be here. I could do this. I'd make new memories here, today. Starting now, I'd no longer associate this place with pain from the past. My old remembrance of it would be replaced with memories of Walker and happiness, and how he was there for me when I stood up to my asshole boss and quit the first job I'd gone to college for.

When I got out of the car, Walker's hands were instantly all over me, one hand tangling in my hair while the other pressed against the small of my back, pulling me into a warm hug. His body closed the space between us and everything in me shot to life. I was hyperaware of every touch of his skin on mine and grateful for the break from my past fears.

"I'm so sorry about your job," he said. "I want to hear everything." He leaned his mouth next to my ear, kissing and nibbling at it between words. "I'll fucking kill your boss if you want me to. I know people," he joked with a flirtatious smile.

At least, I hoped he was joking.

He dipped his chin and looked deeply into my eyes while caressing the nape of my neck. "So, what happened?"

I shook my head, so many issues bombarding me at once. "I don't even know. One second I'm blissfully happy, and the next I'm telling my boss what a raging asshole he is and how much I hate the way he runs his business. Then I quit."

He smiled and gently squeezed the back of my neck. "You were blissfully happy?"

"Really? That's the part you heard?" I pressed my lips together and raised my eyebrows.

Walker let out a big laugh. "No. I heard the rest. I just liked the blissfully happy part the best. Although I gotta admit, you're sort of a badass, babe."

Babe? Sigh.

"Thanks."

I glanced up at the weathered blue-and-white sign in the nearly empty parking lot, and then back toward the old wood entrance where a surfboard hung above it. In all the years that had passed, the café hadn't changed one bit. My stomach lurched at the memories shaking their way loose, and I gripped on to Walker a bit too tight.

"Are you sure you're okay being here? We can leave." His voice softened but I could tell he didn't want to.

Too late, buddy. I'm already here. You've already sent me spiraling back in time.

"I can't believe you don't remember." The light flecks in his eyes sparkled as he looked at me.

"Remember what?"

"You don't remember being here with me before? I wanted to wait until we got inside, but I'm afraid you won't let me get you in there." He smiled wickedly at me, his hand sliding down to stroke my back.

My heart pounded, raced actually, as the memories I'd pushed back since that summer over ten years ago flooded through me. Thoughts of me and my summer crush sitting in the sand, arms wrapped around each other as the sun set. Watching Scotty surf at dawn, and then staying all afternoon when he could, which wasn't often enough since his mom got sick. Saying good-bye here, in the parking lot of what had become "our" café.

And my overly dramatic teenage heart feeling like it broke in two as I had to leave him when the summer ended.

I flipped over, reminding myself that it was time to tan my back, and undid the strap of my bikini top. No one wanted tan lines and I agreed. Propping my head up on top of my fists, I watched Scotty out in the ocean, his arms paddling hard as he moved to catch the oncoming wave. He pushed himself from his knees to his feet in one swift motion, and I envied the smooth, efficient way the surfboard tilted and cut through the water in response to a slight shift in his hips.

Surfing came so easily to him, but when he had tried to teach me yesterday morning, all I accomplished was perfecting my tumbling skills. When I finally did stand on the board in the water, it lasted all of two seconds before my balance slipped away and I landed in the freezing ocean again.

Scotty could have teased me mercilessly, but he didn't. He reminded me that it took most people years to learn how to surf well. Still, I was pissed I hadn't learned in a single day. Ever the perfectionist, I nodded my head at him, but secretly wished I was more athletic.

Ice-cold water droplets rained down my back, pulling me away from yesterday and back to today with a shock. I moved to jump from my towel, but thankfully remembered that my top was untied. Instead I quickly turned my head to the right, seeing Scotty standing above me, ringing out his wet clothes.

"Stop it," I whined as I retied my top.

He placed his cold fingers on my back. "Leave it untied."

My eyes met his. Recognizing the lust-filled hormones raging behind them, I pulled the bow on my top tight and pushed up onto my knees, facing him. "I'm not letting this entire beach see my goodies."

Scotty glanced around from side to side. "Lucky for you, no one's looking. Just me." He folded his arms across his bare chest.

"Nice try," I teased.

With his towel next to mine, Scotty lay down on his side and ran his fingers along my hip. "Need me to rub some suntan lotion on you?"

I swatted at his hand. "Oh my gosh, Scotty! Is sex all you think about?" Only fourteen and still a virgin, sex talk made me nervous. I hadn't felt about any boy in my hometown the way I felt about

Scotty, but I knew the summer was ending soon and most likely, so were we.

He shrugged and closed one eye. "I think about music too." His laugh filled my ears as he leaned down to kiss my lips. "But mostly sex. What can I say? I'm a teenage boy and my loins are needy."

This time it was my own laughter that filled my ears. "Loins? Your loins are needy? Sounds serious. You might want to see a doctor for that," I suggested with a coy smile.

"Wanna play doctor?"

I looked up into Walker's eyes, suddenly realizing why they'd looked so familiar in a more meaningful way. "Oh my God. Oh my God."

My mouth instantly felt dry, as if I'd eaten a bucket filled with sand, and I choked on my words, my thoughts, my memories. My head spun as I tried to keep myself standing upright. It didn't work and I crouched down, wrapping my arms around my knees as I lowered my head, my shoulders wracked with my sobs.

Walker instantly squatted in front of me,

frantically stroking my hair and rubbing my arms, touching me, consoling me in any way he could.

Shaking my head, I looked up, my vision blurred with tears. "Scotty?"

"Scott Walker Rhodes," he corrected gently.

"Is it really you?"

"Was I really that forgettable?" He smirked at me, but I didn't miss the moisture that suddenly filled his eyes.

"It is you, isn't it?" I choked out. "You look so different."

"I finally lost all my baby fat," he said jokingly, but it was true. "And grew about a foot since you last saw me." He flexed his arms, making the muscles press against the sleeves of his shirt as he smiled. "And I've been working out."

I half laughed. It was amazing how much he'd changed since that summer a decade ago. He was much taller now, his body lean and muscular, a far cry from the shorter, pudgier teenage version of him. His hair was now close-cropped and nearly black, very different from the long, wavy sun-bleached dark brown locks that were always falling into his eyes when he was a teenager. And his face was now the face of a man, all chiseled and lean; no remnants of his once-full cheeks remained. But those eyes, they hadn't changed a bit.

We were just kids that summer, but looking at him now, I felt so stupid. I wanted to smack myself for not seeing it before. It seemed so blatantly obvious that the man across from me was Scotty, my summer crush from when I was only fourteen.

Old friends of my family had plans to tour Europe that summer, so they had asked my parents if we would watch the house and take care of their dogs. My parents, both teachers, jumped at the idea of spending the summer in Malibu, and I was overjoyed. Just the thought of spending the whole summer in the Johnsons's huge beach house steps from the ocean thrilled me. I had no idea I'd leave my heart there in the sand when the summer ended.

"I–I can't believe it," I stuttered as I tried to form rational thoughts. "How long have you known? You've always known it was me, haven't you? That was why you were trying to find me." I spoke rapidly, the pieces of the puzzle finally clicking together.

"You look exactly the same, Madison," he said as his fingers twirled my hair. "I mean, you've definitely changed," his gaze roamed along the curves of my body, "but you still look the same."

"Why didn't you say anything at dinner? Or at

my condo?" The wind picked up, blowing my hair into my eyes, and I brushed it back, not wanting to miss any expression on his face while my mind still struggled to put all the pieces together. Not that I was confused any longer, but I did feel overwhelmed.

Walker shrugged, suddenly looking unsure of himself. "I needed the right time. And part of me kept hoping something I would say would trigger a memory and you'd remember on your own."

"I'm really bad with placing faces, and you've changed so much." I shook my head wildly. "Plus I blocked it all out. I'd been too hurt after we lost touch. I forced myself to forget about you, pretend there was no you."

He winced as his breath whooshed out of him. "That's harsh."

"It's reality."

"For you maybe."

I looked up at him. "What does that mean?"

"That means that I never fucking forgot about you." He lifted my chin with his fingers, forcing me to lock eyes with him. "Ever. And the fact that you could erase me from your memory makes me absolutely insane when I could never shake you from mine."

I sucked in an unsure breath, my entire body overloaded with emotion. "I'm not saying that I ever really succeeded. I'm just saying that I tried."

"Stop trying," he said softly, just before his lips pressed against mine.

Love :
intense affection for another person

We had been relaxing on the beach, the sand cool and damp against my bare skin as we'd sat cross-legged next to each other, watching the sun drop through a fiery sky into the ocean.

"I wrote a song about you last night," Scotty said as he wrapped his arm around my waist and attempted to pull me closer.

"About me?" My young heart leaped at the idea of a boy writing a single sentence about me, let alone an entire song.

"Yeah. But it's not finished yet." He planted a damp kiss on my cheek and my face warmed.

"Is it romantic? What's it about?"

Scotty laughed and then shook his head. "Not telling you anything until it's finished."

"Not even a hint? The chorus? A lyric?" I

looked at him, my best puppy-dog eyes on display.

He turned his head to face me and kissed me with all the skill and passion a fifteen-year-old boy could muster. "It's about the first girl I've ever loved. And how I hate the idea of another summer without her."

My eyes instantly filled with tears as the rest of my body went numb. "You love me?"

We hadn't said those words to each other, although God knew I'd loved him for half the summer already. As a young teenage girl, my heart was open and willing for him. It waited to be taken, to be claimed.

His fingers splayed across my hip, digging into my skin as he prepared to say the words I so nervously wanted him to. I knew I loved him, but I never wanted to say it first. What if he hadn't loved me back? I couldn't stand the humiliation. It would take everything in me to not pack my bags and beg my parents to take me back to the valley.

"I think I do," he said. "You've made this summer perfect. You're perfect."

In that moment I had known I'd never find another boy quite like Scotty. His mom being sick had made him more vulnerable and sensitive. I had felt that every moment I spent with him, I was seeing a side of Scotty that no one else got to see.

"I think I love you too," I said breathlessly.

But I didn't "think" I loved him. I knew.

Interrupting my thoughts, Walker leaned his forehead against mine, dragging me back to the present. "I almost had a heart attack on that platform when I first saw you at the concert. I kept trying to convince myself that it wasn't you. That it couldn't be you. But deep down, I knew. And that headband, the way it sparkled above your head, drew my eyes to you. You looked so beautiful, like you stepped out of a fairy tale."

I plopped down on the ground, feeling light-headed from squatting so long, and scooted closer to him. My eyes wanted to drown in him as my brain struggled to memorize every feature so that I'd never forget again. How could I have ever forgotten in the first place?

"Do you have any idea how hard it was for me to keep singing after I saw you?" He barked out a laugh and shook his head. "Holy shit, babe, I wanted to jump off that platform, take you in my arms, and run away. You know, give the tabloids something to really talk about!"

I laughed for the first time that day. It felt good to smile, even if my thoughts were racing at a breakneck pace.

"And after the show. When I realized you didn't leave your number like I'd asked, I fucking lost it."

"Lost it how?"

He shrugged and rolled his eyes. "I might have broken some things. No big deal."

I looked away, suddenly embarrassed. "I thought you asked for every girl's number. I mean, I just assumed you wanted to add me to your never-ending list of conquests. It pissed me off when you asked."

Walker leaned forward and wiped the tears from my cheek, then cupped my face with his hand. "Only my girl would get pissed off when a celebrity asks for her number."

My girl?

Lord, have mercy. I promise to hang on to this boy and never let him go if you let me have him. I don't even need him wrapped up with a bow. I'll take him just the way he is. Please.

"No number," he went on. "And still no last name. But I was older this time and had more resources. There was no way I was letting you slip out of my life twice." He leaned toward me, his lips meeting mine, and I melted into him, wanting to forget everything that ever existed before he sang his way back into my life.

Walker's words and actions caused more tears to fall. I'd been so heartbroken after the summer ended and we eventually lost touch. No one had ever warned me that first loves could have such an impact on you. I wasn't sure I'd ever fully recovered, although I'd definitely tried.

Sitting here now in the parking lot of this café, pain shot through my chest with each breath I took, a clear reminder that the scars left by those lost first loves never truly heal. At least, not without permanent damage.

His warm breath rustled my hair. "I'm sorry about losing touch."

"I was just thinking about that. What happened? I tried your cell, but it was disconnected or no longer in service." I remembered the robotic female voice on that recording as clear as day, taunting me as if she knew something I didn't.

He picked up one of my hands and pressed it to his lips, then looked into my eyes. "I took my cell phone with me everywhere. I never wanted to miss a call from you because I never knew when one was coming. I even brought it to the beach when I surfed." He glanced up at the sky, as if pulling memories from the clouds. "It got wet one day after I'd been in the water. Completely fried the thing. It wouldn't even turn on."

"And you never got a new one? You couldn't call me from your house phone?" I asked, suddenly feeling fourteen again, recalling pacing the floor in front of our home phone while I willed it to ring.

"I didn't have your phone number written down anywhere. It was only in my cell phone. And yes, I got a new one. Eventually. But my parents made me work around the house to earn the money to pay for it, so I didn't get another phone for almost three months. But your number was gone forever by that time."

"I left you voice mails," I said softly. "So many voice mails. Until your phone stopped taking them." The memories still felt fresh, my teenage self crying into the phone and asking him why he wasn't calling me back. Thinking back, it seemed like I was nothing if not overdramatic. But I remembered being so truly heartbroken at the time, I'd convinced myself that I would never get over him. Eventually I had, but not before crying until the tears would no longer fall. Every emotion, especially love, was so amplified when you were a kid. Hell, I didn't even know what love truly was at that age, but I thought I felt it for him.

"Those messages broke my damn heart, Madison. Especially when you never left your phone number in any of them. I heard them all back-to-back when I got my new phone turned on. It took everything in me to not smash the damn thing to pieces."

"That would have been counterproductive," I teased, trying to lighten the mood.

"When I got to the last voice mail you left me, I knew in my heart that you'd given up." He squeezed my hand.

I sighed. "I think I actually said that in my message, if I remember right."

"You did. But I didn't want it to be true. And you never called again."

"Well, you stopped calling back. I just assumed the worst. You know, that you were sick of me calling you and that's why you changed your number. Or that you found someone new. But it all went back to you being over me."

His face pinched with pain. "I hate hearing that. You have no idea how much I hate hearing that right now. I tried to find you. I looked everywhere I could but there was no Facebook then. No social media like there is now to stalk people effectively."

"There was MySpace," I reminded him.

"But you didn't have one."

"You didn't either." I recalled a conversation we'd had on the beach one afternoon where we confessed that we weren't obsessed with computers like our friends were.

He laughed and my face flushed. "Not that I would have had much luck trying to find Madison from the valley."

I listened to the surf breaking nearby and felt numb, as if everything inside me had disappeared. I was certain my heart wasn't beating, my lungs weren't working, and whatever else in there was either broken or gone. This was all so surreal, I still couldn't believe it was happening.

"I can't believe it's you. I can't believe you're here." I turned my head to look out at the ocean across the sand. "We made so many memories together at this beach."

He nodded. "It's why I brought you here. To this day, I can't come here and not think of you."

"It's why I didn't want to come," I said softly, still struggling to regain some sense of composure.

His eyebrows lifted and his expression brightened. "Was that why? I wondered, but of course I couldn't ask."

"I never come here. The last time I was here was with you. That day we said good-bye."

"Don't remind me. That was one of the hardest days of my life. Even now, when I add up the days in my life that have royally sucked, like this morning, it still ranks up there at the top."

"You're leaving?" Scotty had asked, his hazel eyes etched with pain that even as a teenager I could recognize.

My heart had constricted so tightly I could barely speak, so I had nodded instead as tears flowed freely down my sun-kissed cheeks. The breeze whipped my hair, causing strands to stick to the wet tracks on my face.

"Don't cry, Madison. We'll still talk. I'll call you every day. And we'll figure out a way to see each other again. I promise." His words were insistent and determined, as though he believed them.

"I don't want to go," I choked out through my sobs. My hands reached out to stroke back the wavy sun-streaked strands that the breeze stirred in front of his eyes.

Scotty wiped at my tears, plucking my own stuck strands free and tucking them behind my ear before pulling me into a hard hug. "I don't want you to go either. I'm not ready to say good-bye."

"I'll never be ready," I said solemnly.

"This has been the best summer of my life. You hear me? The best."

Reluctant to leave, I pulled away from his embrace. "I have to go. My parents are waiting for me."

"I–I," he stuttered before looking down at the sand. "I love you."

"I love you too." The words slid effortlessly from my teenage lips.

"This isn't done between us. You and me," he said, his breathing ragged. "We're not over. You believe me, don't you?"

I had nodded, wanting with all my heart to believe his words. Then he had kissed me. His tongue had stroked desperately in and out of my mouth, his awkward and rushed movements proof of his inexperience.

The memory faded as Walker's voice filled my ears and his face came into view. "God, Madison. I looked for you. The following summer." His eyes glistened, and I knew I'd lose it even more if he cried.

I willed him not to. Not here. Not in this moment when I so desperately needed to pull it together and not fall apart.

"You never went back to the beach, did you?" he asked.

I thought back, recalling how distraught I'd been when I lost contact with him. How desperately I wanted to be in touch with him and how hopeless I'd felt. My mom and best friend both told me to forget him. They insisted that he'd long since forgotten about me and I needed to do the same. I didn't want to believe them, but I eventually stopped ignoring the obvious message his silence contained.

By the time the following summer came around and we ended up on the beaches of Malibu, I made sure to never go near *our* beach again.

I shook my head. "I couldn't. I didn't want to go back there. Too many memories. Plus, my best friend had me convinced that you had moved on. She asked me how I'd feel if I saw you with someone else. I knew it would kill me, so I never risked it."

"Actually, I did the exact opposite."

I leaned toward him, looking up into his eyes. "What do you mean?" As his thumb idly circled the skin on my hand, I thought about how I never wanted it to stop. I never wanted him to stop touching me. Ever.

"Almost every day the next summer, I went to that particular spot at the beach looking for you. I was obsessed, wanting so badly to see you again, that I convinced myself you'd know I was waiting. That you'd be able to sense me there." He paused. "I needed to find you, but you never came. And eventually I stopped going."

Shocked, I leaned away from him, my back pressing into the hard steel of my car as I allowed the realization of his words to sink in. He'd gone back to the beach to look for me? He had wanted to see me again?

"I figured you were done with me," I whispered. "Forgotten all about me. We were just kids."

Walker tipped my face up and snared my gaze with his. "I could never forget you. You've always held a piece of my heart, Madison."

More tears fell and I quickly brushed them away with the back of my hand.

"Let's go inside and eat," he suggested. "Think you can handle being back in our café?" He pushed himself from off the ground and extended a hand to me.

"As long as I'm with you, I think I can handle anything." I reached for his hand and he pulled me up effortlessly before yanking me against him.

"Looks like you'll be unstoppable because I'm never leaving your side again." His hands splayed across my back as he dipped his head so his lips could meet mine.

My body leaned into his as my mouth opened, accepting him, wanting him. I reached around his neck and lightly raked my fingernails down the length of it before stopping at his shoulders. Our tongues took turns moving from one mouth to the other, every stroke, every touch making our hearts beat faster.

Walker pulled back. "We need to stop or I'm going to end up throwing you down right here in the parking lot and having my way with you," he said with a teasing tone.

I burst out laughing. "The press would have a field day! Could you imagine? Let's go eat. Suddenly I'm starving."

"Me too." He licked his lips. "But not for food."

The café's teenage hostess had a mini breakdown before seating us, fanning her face with her hand and shakily asking Walker for his autograph. My heart, which had miraculously found its way back into my chest, swelled with appreciation. I'd been absent for so many years from Walker's life, but I suddenly felt like I hadn't missed a day.

Once we were seated in our booth, I looked over at him, so proud of the man he had become. And I knew his mother would be too. Now it made sense why he had asked me last night if I remembered her being sick. Of course I had. His mom had been diagnosed the summer we met. I'd always thought that going through that together had bonded us in a deeper way. I never truly imagined how right I was.

I had been sitting in the sand playing fetch with one of the Johnsons's dogs when I'd found myself mesmerized by the surfers in the water. The way they paddled out on their boards, moving in a particular direction before I even noticed any inkling of a wave forming, was beautiful to watch. When they would rise to their feet and maneuver the board like it was attached to them, cutting through waves doing tricks I couldn't even imagine doing, I wanted to stand up and applaud.

One of the younger guys rode a small chopper until it ended at the shoreline. He tucked his board under his arm and jogged up to sit in the sand next to me. I almost asked him what he wanted when I noticed a pile of clothing sitting there.

"Hey," he said, and I turned to see the hottest pair of hazel eyes staring back at me.

"Hey, yourself."

"Local or tourist?" he asked as he lowered the zipper from his wetsuit and shimmied it halfway down his body, revealing his bare chest.

"Um…" I hesitated, unsure of how to answer. I wasn't from Malibu, but I wasn't a tourist either.

"Do you live here or are you from out of state?" A towel now sat wrapped tightly around his

waist as he pulled the rest of his wetsuit free.

Hiding my nervousness, I looked away as I said, "I'm from the valley, but we're staying here all summer."

From the corner of my eye, I watched as his tanned feet stepped into a pair of board shorts and he pulled them up just as the towel fell away. "Which house?"

"The Johnsons's." I offered up the information freely, not pausing to consider whether it was safe to tell him.

"Cool. I live two doors down." He pulled a black T-shirt over his head and tossed his wetsuit across his board.

My face lit up at the idea of having met a friend already. And the fact that he was a totally hot guy didn't hurt either.

"What's your name?"

"Madison. My name's Madison."

"I'm Scott. I'll see you around, Madison from the valley," he shouted over his shoulder as he carried his surfboard away.

"Wanna stay and hang out?" I called out, hoping he'd stop walking and come back to me.

He stopped and turned around. "I can't. My mom's sick and I need to get home. Just wanted to catch some waves before she woke up." Then he waved and turned to head home.

"Oh, okay. See you around."

I didn't realize at the time that his mom was terminally ill. Being so young, I'd just assumed he meant she had the flu, or something harmless like that. It never occurred to me to think otherwise. A typical teenage girl, I was naïve and unaware.

My throat parched, I reached for the water on the table and downed the entire glass.

"You have a thing with water." Walker smirked, his eyes searching mine, and I wanted to climb across the table and hop into his lap. "I still write songs about that summer, you know." He bit his lip and my mind suddenly filled with all the naughty things I could do to that lip. And all the naughty things I *would* do to it.

My overactive imagination snapped back to reality with a thud. "What did you just say? Which songs?"

A rosy color crept over his cheeks as he looked

down at the crumpled napkin he held. "'The One Who Got Away' and 'That Summer,' obviously," he said as he tore at the napkin, placing bits of crinkled paper around the table as his eyes avoided mine. "And then, 'Where'd She Go and Disappear.'"

I almost choked on my water at the mention of the last song. I was obsessed with it when it came out, hitting REPEAT on my iPod constantly so I could hear the haunting lyrics and melody one more time.

She said good-bye that day
But I never knew she meant it
I always wanted her to stay
But the winds of change carried her away
Forever in my heart
That girl and I will never be far apart
But until we meet again
I'll keep searching for her and then
My world will fall back into place
A moment in time I can never erase
It happened just like I feared
She went and disappeared
Disappeared

*How do you go on when your love has
Disappeared*

"I love that song the most," I admitted.

His eyes met mine. "Which one?"

"'Disappeared.' It's always been my favorite."

His eyebrows rose and he laughed. "Well, it's about you, so I guess that's fitting. You never had any idea that the songs were about you?"

Teasingly, I slapped at his shoulder. "Walker! How could I ever think that? I didn't even know who you were!"

Calling him Walker set me back for a moment. I'd gotten used to calling him that, but seeing him now, he was Scotty *and* he was Walker, all wrapped up in one delicious package. I would always have the memories of Scotty, but it was the man, Walker, that I was so incredibly attracted to, now that I could see him clearly for who he really was.

He shook his head at me. "But the lyrics, Madison, they're so obvious. They're filled with memories that only you and I shared. You never thought? Not even in the back of your mind?"

I shrugged. "Not really. I mean, I've always loved your music. But I never once thought that any of the songs were about me. Especially not with your reputation."

He snorted. "I really need to clear up this whole bad-boy persona bit."

I leaned over and smiled as I grabbed his hand. "I couldn't agree with you more."

"You'll help, right?" He tugged at my hand. "Say you'll be in every paparazzi photograph with me from here on out. Anytime I'm with a girl, it will be you."

I coughed and raised an eyebrow. So many things were happening at such a rushed pace. I longed to scream that I'd never leave his side again—that he could superglue us together for all I cared—but that thought alone scared the hell out of me. My lustful feelings for him terrified the logical side of me. The whole situation was surreal, and my head refused to wrap itself around the intensity that my heart pumped out. Was there a way to get both sides of me on the same page?

A thousand fears suddenly seemed at home inside my already flustered body. It was too much at once. Being here with him in this café, making plans for the future and thinking about the past; I thought I might lose it.

"Walker. I need to get out of here."

"Let's go." He bumped his knees against the table and shot to his feet.

"I meant that I need to get out of here. Alone," I said as my body stayed still in the booth.

"Alone?" Panic flashed across his face and my stomach dropped.

"Just let me process all of this, okay? My life has turned completely inside out in the last twenty-four hours, and I just need..." I shook my head. "I just need some time."

"Away from me?" he asked. "I just fucking found you and you want to get rid of me already?"

"I'm not trying to get rid of you."

Not really.

He reached for my hand before pulling us through the empty restaurant to the hostess stand. "Sorry," he told her, "but we're not staying. Can you let our waitress know?"

The hostess, clearly still flustered, smiled and nodded as she stared at Walker wide-eyed as he pushed the doors open and strode across the parking lot to my car.

"Don't do this, Madison. Don't push me away."

I turned toward him and winced at seeing the pain so clearly etched between his furrowed brows. "Walker, please. I just need to be alone." I squeezed my eyes shut and pressed my palms against them.

Warm arms wrapped around me and I shook my head, my eyes still covered.

"Look at me," he said, his tone soft and pleading.

I lowered my hands slowly and opened my eyes to watch his face as he struggled to find the words. Seeing the emotions that battled behind his eyes, I tried to pull away from his grip, but he only held me tighter.

"I don't want you to go," he admitted between labored breaths.

I sighed. "I know you don't. But this is something I need to do. For me. I just need some time. Th-this"—I struggled to find my voice as well—"this is a lot for me to go through in one afternoon."

He released me and paced in the small space between our cars, walking back and forth with his head in his hands. I watched him and waited. My need for space wasn't meant to hurt or confuse him, but I needed to figure things out. He'd had more than ten minutes to process seeing me, knowing who I was and putting all that information together. I needed the same courtesy.

In the span of a few hours I'd quit my job, and

then found out that Walker Rhodes was Scotty, the first boy I'd ever loved. I was abruptly unemployed, thrust into past memories that haunted me, and I wasn't sure which freaked me out more.

Walker stopped pacing and leaned his body next to mine, our shoulders touching. The feeling I experienced at his closeness underscored the complete conflict of my emotions—how I wanted his hands all over me, yet at the same time needed to be as far away from them as possible. My heart stitched itself back together in his presence, as my head fell apart in jigsaw-puzzle pieces. How could two instincts inside one body be at such complete odds with each other?

The silence lingering between us virtually strangled me and I didn't know what else to say to him. Finally he said, "I can't lose you again," and I almost took back every word I had spoken in the last few minutes.

Almost.

"Walker," I said, turning my body so I could face him. I wanted to reassure him that everything would be okay, but I didn't want to lie. My internal conflict raged within me and I simply needed space. "I'm gonna go."

I pushed past him and opened the door to my

car. He stepped aside to allow me through, and when I looked up into his eyes, I winced at the pain I saw there. "I'll call you tomorrow."

"Tomorrow?" he asked through gritted teeth, as though I'd told him I'd call him next year. "No. Call me later. Call me tonight. I'll be a fucking wreck."

I chewed on my bottom lip before shaking my head and repeating, "I'll call you tomorrow."

As I stepped on the gas to pull away, he didn't try to stop me and I didn't try to stay.

> **Girlfriend:**
> a favorite female companion, female friend

Driving away from Walker had been more difficult than I anticipated, but it needed to be done. I craved the peace and tranquility of my condo, and I desperately wanted to talk to Keri. This was too much to deal with alone. I needed my girlfriend. Walker and I hadn't even touched on the fact that I'd lost my job earlier. My head was swimming with fears...fear for my professional life, and suddenly fears for my personal life as well.

When I finally pulled into my spot at the condo, I was reminded that the paparazzi had me on their radar as a few men loitered around the street, jumping out of their cars the second I arrived. Determined, I gathered my things and shook my head as I walked through them, refusing to look in their direction when they screamed my name and shouted stupid questions.

I had never realized before how hard it was not to look at someone when they call you by name. It's like an ingrained response to at least make eye contact or acknowledge that you heard them. Keeping my head down, I unlocked the door and closed it tight behind me before heading out the back toward the far stairwell. Without Walker there to block me, I had no desire to be filmed as I waited for the elevator.

My phone beeped and I glanced down at it. The text message was from Walker:

IF YOU CALL ME TONIGHT INSTEAD OF TOMORROW, I WON'T HOLD IT AGAINST YOU. YOU CAN EVEN CALL ME NOW. I PROMISE I WON'T MIND.

Unlocking the front door with a sigh, I stepped inside and pressed my back against it, sliding all the way down to the floor. Instead of focusing on everything I'd learned about Walker today and his latest text message, I forced my mind to deal with the fact that I'd quit my job and had very little money in savings. I knew I'd be able to get by for at least a few months, but I needed to get a new job as soon as possible. And in this town, it wasn't going to be easy.

Competition for everything here was fierce; especially in the entertainment industry. Feeling like I had royally fucked myself, I pushed up from the floor and headed into my bedroom, typing a text message to Keri on my way.

PLEASE TELL ME YOU AREN'T WORKING LATE. I NEED YOU.

I wasn't sure what else to say without freaking her out or losing it myself, so I kept it short and simple. She would assume I was still at the office as well. But I wasn't. Because I quit my job today, called my boss names, and walked out the door. My phone chirped and I looked down.

IS EVERYTHING OK? WILL BE HOME AT NORMAL TIME. I'LL BRING FOOD.

Thank God. The mere mention of food sent my stomach growling. I needed a distraction. Something to keep me occupied until Keri walked through the door, otherwise I might go insane. Heading into the bathroom, I turned on the water and ran a hot bath. I couldn't remember the last time I'd soaked in the tub, but I needed to relax.

Turned out that taking a bath had been the perfect escape. My mind slowed as I let the warm water surround and soothe me. Before I knew it, Keri scared the crap out of me by barging through the front door yelling for me.

"I'm here! Where are you?"

Water splashed all around as I jumped up and pulled the plug free of the drain. Over the gurgling sound of water being sucked away, I yelled, "I'm in the bathroom. Be out in a sec!"

Wrapping the towel around me, I scooted from the bathroom to my bedroom so I could get into comfortable clothes. A pair of yoga pants and sweatshirt later, I waltzed into the living room where the smell of food invaded my senses.

"I'm starving. Thank you so much for getting dinner." I looked down at the pizza, the order of chicken wings, salad, and garlic knots. "Uh, did you think you were feeding an army? You know just the two of us live here, right?"

Keri looked over at me with a wary look. I rarely texted her asking when she'd be home, and it was even more rare for me to tell her I needed her.

"I didn't know what you'd be in the mood for,"

she said, "so I sort of got a little of everything. I can eat it all myself, though, if you wanna bitch about it?"

I smiled. "First of all, I'd pay a hundred bucks to see you eat all this food yourself. Second, thank you. The pizza looks perfect. I need some comfort food."

She looked at me with disapproval. "Only you would consider pizza comfort food."

I laughed. "More like me and the rest of America. What the heck do you consider comfort food?"

"Grilled cheese, soup, macaroni and cheese," she rattled out off the top of her head.

"And pizza," I added.

After grabbing a slice of pizza, Keri scooped some salad onto her plate and moved toward the couch where I had just sat last night with Walker. "Get over here and tell me what's going on."

I reached for two slices of the greasy, cheesy goodness, grabbed a diet soda from the fridge, and sat next to her on the couch. Wondering where I should start first, I decided to drop the bomb about my quitting. I'd get to Walker later.

"I quit my job today."

She half choked on her food. "You what? Why? What happened?" Before I could respond, she asked, "Oh gosh, what did that asshole do? Does it have to do with Walker? It does, doesn't it? Everything he did to you is so illegal and he knows it. He's not an idiot. Ah, this business makes me crazy sometimes!"

"Are you finished?" I asked between bites.

She eyed the ceiling like she was contemplating saying more, then shrugged. "For now."

After I gave Keri a play-by-play of what happened with Jayson this morning, she raised her hand in the air for a high-five and I slapped it, feeling empowered. "You're my fucking hero!"

I laughed and it felt good. "Well, I don't feel like a hero. I mean, I know that what I did was the right thing to do for me. But now I'm jobless, so I feel more like an unemployed schmuck than anything else."

"Being unemployed is a minor detail," she said as she waved off my objections.

"Minor detail? You know how hard it was for me to even get that job without having strings pulled. How am I going to get another? It's tough out there!"

"You can come work for my dad."

"No, thank you. Maybe as a last resort." I loved that she was this thoughtful, but I had no interest working in the movie industry. Working with the talent and negotiating on their behalf was definitely the side of the business I wanted to be on.

"Bitch," she snapped out with a half laugh.

"You know production isn't my thing. It's your thing. But thank you."

"Okay, but the offer still stands. Not that you'll need it. I have complete faith in your abilities."

"In my abilities to tell my boss off and blacklist myself from every agency within a fifty-mile radius?" I took another bite of my idea of comfort food and swallowed.

"Not happening." She leaned forward and shook her head. "Oh my God! Wait! How am I forgetting about last night? Girl, you need to tell me all about your date with Walker and how the hell the two of you ended up here!"

I smiled and a quick laugh escaped from within me at her enthusiasm. My brain didn't miss the way my heart sped up at the mention of his name, either. "I don't even know where to start with that one."

"There can't be that much to tell. It was only last night." She reached for her drink and took a swig before tilting her head at me with a glimmer in her eye. "What aren't you telling me?"

My back sank into the cushions of the couch until I could squish myself against it no more. I sighed. "Last night was a disaster. I was a total bitch at dinner, and I let it slip that I was only there because Jayson wanted him to sign with our agency."

"Madison in bitch mode is quite entertaining. I like it," Keri said with a knowing grin.

"So he told me to leave. Straight up pointed and everything, and told me to leave the restaurant."

Her hand flew over her gaping mouth. "Shut up."

"Seriously. It was so embarrassing. I walked outside and the paparazzi fucking swarmed me. They were yelling my name and asking my about my job and it was madness."

"How'd they even—" She stopped mid-thought. "Jayson told them."

I nodded before continuing. "Walker rushed out after me, hopped in my car, and refused to leave. He told me he wanted to talk to me. We had nowhere to go and that's how we ended up here."

"He wanted to talk to you? Talk to you about what? And he wouldn't get out of your car? I think I love this guy." She laughed, clearly having a great time at my expense.

"Let me finish."

She scowled at me and muttered, "Then finish."

Swallowing another gulp of soda, I placed the can between my legs and buried my head in my hands. "Okay," I started, looking up at my clueless friend. "So whatever, we're here last night. It's fine. We had a great time. He kissed me, blah blah. Let's just fast forward to today."

"He kissed you?" Keri's eyes widened to the size of saucers. "I want to hear about that!"

"Hold on!" I shouted back at her. "So after I quit, I called Walker from the parking garage."

"Wait! You called Walker first?" Her hand smacked down on the arm of the couch, sending dust particles into the air. "He was the first person you called?"

The realization of her statement hit me like a weighted gym bag. "Yeah, I guess." I shrugged as I tried to slough it off. "Anyway, Keri, just listen." She folded her arms across her chest as I tried to navigate my words carefully. "So he asks me to meet him at this café. And it's like the one place in Malibu I never go because it reminds me of the guy I met that one summer."

"Oh, your Malibu guy, right?" Keri brought it

up so naturally, as if this were a subject we discussed on a daily basis. I think we talked about it one time, but Keri had a memory like an elephant. She remembered *everything*.

I fast-forwarded to the point where I got to the café. Keri's face was a mixture of confusion and excitement as she listened to me spill the details of my afternoon, which felt like it happened eons ago instead of mere hours.

"So I step out of the car and we're talking and he can't take it anymore. He confesses to me who he is. And then I feel like such a fucking idiot for not ever seeing it before because really, Keri? Even though he doesn't look the same"—I paused for affect—"he still totally looks the same!"

"You're not saying..." Keri scrunched up her face, and then the light bulb came on. "Oh my God, you're not saying... Walker's n-not," she stuttered, then her eyes got huge. "He's your surfer summer love guy?"

"How insane is that? I mean, this kind of thing just... Does. Not. Happen," I said, my head still trying to comprehend the events and correlate them with my life now.

"But his name wasn't Walker? I mean, even you would remember a name like that."

"I guess Walker's his middle name. When I met him that summer, he went by Scotty."

"That's right! Scotty the surfer!" She smiled, clearly remembering more of my story. "So you didn't recognize him at all? Ever? Nothing about him has ever struck you as familiar? I know how bad you are with faces, but really?" Poor Keri looked like her head was spinning with a million questions that I'd already asked myself earlier.

"The only thing about him that was familiar were his eyes, but I thought I just recognized them because of his being a celebrity. And of course, now I feel like I should have always known because even though he's changed so much since then, he's still totally him. You know?"

She shook her head. "I want to yell at you because we've seen him so many times online and on TV, but I'm also the girl who has to remind you where we know people from everywhere we go. You really, really suck at faces. But Walker Rhodes? How do you forget that face, no matter how much you suck at remembering people?"

It was so frustrating, having to defend myself when she knew how horrible I was with faces. "It was over ten years ago, and we were just kids. He looked totally different then. Keri, he was just a boy, but now he's a grown-ass man. A really hot, grown-ass man."

Keri jumped up from the couch and started pacing in small circles. "Madison. You do realize how amazing this is, don't you? This is the kind of thing they write movies about. I'm going to write a movie about this. Yeah. Maybe I'll become a screenwriter and your story will be the first one I write."

"Keri!" I practically screeched.

"Don't worry, I'm kidding. Kind of," she said as she scrunched up her face while she thought. "It's not a horrible idea. You'd know the writer, so the story would be incredibly flattering on your behalf."

"Oh my gosh, shut up!"

Her pacing continued and I swore I could see the wheels turning in her mind. "So, did he know? That night at the concert, when he pulled you onstage?"

I nodded. "He said he recognized me right away."

"This all makes so much sense. I mean, the way he's been acting. The way he was with you at his concert. All of it." Keri sat back down on the couch, her hands folded in her lap. "So, how do you feel?"

I sucked in a breath and tried to stop the smile from forming on my lips. "I can't believe it's him. I can't believe he recognized me. When I think about him, I feel like he's always been a part of me. You know?"

A smile spread across her face. "I don't think we ever get over our first loves completely. We move on, of course, but I think a part of them is always with us."

"I think if you would have asked me that question a few days ago, my answer would have been completely different. I would have told you I was fine, and that he rarely, if ever, crossed my mind."

"And now?"

"I can't imagine ever not being with him again." The words slipped out before my mind had the sense to stop them. "But that's crazy, right?"

"It is." Keri reached out a hand and placed it on my knee. "But it kind of isn't. You two have a past that bonds you. No one can tell you how to feel about it."

"It's so weird, though. Seeing him and realizing who he is...there is just this immediate comfort and trust. I know there's a lot we don't know about each other anymore, and I'm sure we've both changed, but when I look at him, all I see is the boy I fell in love with at the beach all those years ago." I wiped at the lone tear that fell from my eye.

"I get that," Keri said as she nodded. "This is a stupid example, but it's like when I go to a club and I happen to run into someone that I knew from high school. Sometimes I want to be around that person because it feels like I've known them forever. And there's this connection there that this person knows me differently than anyone else in the room does."

"Even if that's not entirely true?" I asked, for her sake as much as my own.

"Yeah, I guess. It's just more of a feeling of familiarity and comfort."

"So then, what if all I'm feeling is exactly that and it's not real? What if I'm just feeling lost in the moment, or all caught up in the sweetness of our innocent past?"

Keri moved her hand and smacked my knee. "Is that what you really think it is?"

I looked away. "Not really."

"Thank God, 'cause I didn't want to have to punch you. Stop being dumb and call the guy. Or better yet, invite him over so I can make an ass of myself again."

Chuckling, I smiled at her. "I told him I'd call him tomorrow."

"Well, is that him who keeps blowing up your phone?" She looked pointedly at my phone, referring to the few times it had lit up during our conversation.

I reached for the phone and glanced at it. "Text messages."

Her lips curved into a sly smile. "I'm not going to tell you what to do."

"Yes, you are."

"You're right, I am." She sucked in a breath. "You better text him back. This is Walker Rhodes we're talking about. Which, speaking of..." She raised a hand in the air and crinkled her brow. "What about this reputation of his? Please tell me you asked him about it, because I don't think I could take my roomie being tabloid fodder. And you know you will be. How are you going to handle that?"

"I'll be fine. I don't care about the tabloids." Sitting here in the safety of my living room, imagining potential future tabloid articles didn't bother me. I figured I could handle anything they dished out, if they dished at all.

"You say that now."

I nodded in agreement. "I do. So when I start freaking out, remind me that I don't care."

She giggled. "Done."

I filled her in on all the details of Walker's past and the things he had confessed to me about his friends and his mom. She nodded vigorously, insisting that it all made perfect and total sense. Keri hopped on the Walker train before tickets were even available for purchase. She loved this entire scenario which was now my life, and refused to feel bad about that fact.

"Honestly, Madison, I know you may not see it right now, but this is all pretty amazing. Your story is romantic as hell, and when people find out about it, they're all going to storm the beaches of Malibu in search of their own summer romances. I couldn't have scripted anything this perfect if I tried. No one could."

I closed my eyes and smiled. "Trust me, Ker, I think it's pretty amazing myself. Part of me still can't believe it."

"Well, believe it."

After giving her a squeeze good night and thanking her for buying dinner, I stretched my arms over my head and sauntered into the kitchen, discarding my trash before heading toward my room.

"Madison?" Keri's voice made me pause and I angled my head back toward her. "You'll get another job. I'll help you look, okay? And I'll talk to my dad to see if he knows anyone who needs an assistant."

"Thank you." I pursed my lips together as I continued down the dimly lit hall, the realization that I could only deal with one thing at a time hitting me square in the face.

"Now go get your man!" Her voice trailed down the hall and I went to my room, slamming the door shut behind me.

Glancing at the clock, I noted the time; a little after ten p.m. It was too late to look for work, but it wasn't too late to deal with Walker. My heart flipped inside my chest. I could feel it dancing away—probably to one of his songs—as I pressed the buttons to call his number.

He answered on the second ring. "Are you trying to kill me?"

"What are you talking about?" I giggled into the phone.

"I told you that I'd be going nuts until I talked to you. You're driving me crazy."

"And I told you I'd call you tomorrow. It's not even tomorrow yet."

"It's almost tomorrow."

I laughed and glanced at my clock again. "Not even close."

"You haven't answered a single text."

"I was talking to Keri about everything."

Walker's tone turned even more serious. "Listen to me, Madison. I can't have you running away from me. I know you needed some time today to process and work through everything, but don't push me away. I don't like it. I want to be the one you run to, not the one you run from."

My defenses prickled at his bossiness. I didn't normally like being told what to do, but in this case, I found myself liking his demands. "I'm not running away from you. I just needed a minute to work through my own head."

"You took hours."

"You're being ridiculous." I closed my eyes and shook my head, secretly enjoying how much he wanted me.

"No. What's ridiculous is how fucking crazy I am about you still. Even after all these years. The moment I saw you in the dark with that sparkly thing on your head, all of these buried emotions came rushing back. It's cheesy and I sound like a girl, but it's the truth. I've never once forgotten about you. Not completely." He blew out a breath. "And now that you're back in my life, I don't plan on letting you get away from me again."

"There's so much we don't know about each other," I admitted, one of my fears working its way to the surface. *What if he's not the same? What if I don't like who he's become? What if he doesn't like me the way he thinks he does?*

"That's true. But I want to get to know every single thing about you, to hear about every moment I've missed. I want inside your brain, your thoughts, your heart, your pants."

A loud laugh ripped from my chest at his last want. "You would."

"I'm male."

"I'm aware."

"So, when can I see you?"

I smiled, my heart skipping a beat with his words. "Tomorrow. I'll come to you."

"Tomorrow can't come soon enough. I'll call you in the morning."

Before I could respond, he added, "And Madison, don't overthink this. Okay? Don't overthink us or our situation or our past. Just listen to your feelings and don't try to stop them with logic. Promise me that."

How the hell could he be so in tune with me already? Maybe he was that good with women in general and I was just overly typical? Whatever it was, he was right on the money.

"I promise."

"Good. Now go to sleep and then get your sweet ass over here."

I huffed out, "You sure are bossy. I don't remember you being so bossy when we were teenagers."

His voice lowered to practically a growl. "I'm not bossy, I just know what I want. You're lucky I'm not outside your door right now begging you to let me in. You're lucky I'm willing to wait until tomorrow to see you."

"Fame's changed you," I said with a laugh.

"No, it hasn't. Good night, Sparkles." My phone lit up and I pulled it away from my face to see that he had ended the call.

He acted so sure, so determined, and I'd be damned if I wasn't completely turned on by it all. Walker was so different from any of the other guys I dated in the past. They all acted like they were trying to be what you wanted them to be, or they put up such a fake front it was almost sickening to be around.

There was nothing fake about Walker Rhodes. The question was, what was I going to do about it?

Completion: the quality or state of being complete

I woke up bright and early the next morning, my body's natural alarm clock prodding me awake, used to getting up at this ungodly hour for work. My mind raced with thoughts about how I shouldn't be heading over to Walker's house; instead, I should be spending my time looking for a new job.

I sucked in a long, cleansing breath and slowly released it, determined to ignore logic for today. Allowing myself one day of reprieve to spend with Walker before I started hunting for a new job wouldn't be a bad thing. I could survive that.

The shrill reminder beep of my cell phone diverted my attention. Who texted this early in the morning?

ARE YOU AWAKE YET?

I smiled immediately before I noted the time. Walker had sent me this text message over an hour ago. Didn't the guy ever sleep? Pressing my head against my pillow, I pulled the covers up to my chest and snuggled back into place. I groggily pressed in Walker's number and waited as excited nerves ticked through me.

"Finally," he breathed into the phone.

"It's six in the morning."

"I couldn't sleep. Are you coming over? Do you want me to come get you?"

"I'll come to you. Text me the directions."

Following the directions Walker sent me, my thoughts bounced the entire time between getting lost and not getting there soon enough. I turned left at the signal light near one of the most popular beach entrances in Malibu, and headed around the bend in the road, passing the public beach on the right and cliffs fronted with restaurants on the left. My car headed up a steep and winding cliff road before reaching the flattened top.

Glancing to my right, I took a moment to appreciate the breathtaking ocean view. This was the kind of view that dreams were made of. Very expensive dreams.

I drove slowly down the street, passing houses on either side of the road. If I didn't know any better, I'd swear I was in a regular suburban neighborhood. But I did know better. The address Walker provided came into view and I put on my blinker, pulling into the gated driveway. Punching in the code he'd given me onto a large silver keypad, I watched as the black iron gates sprang to life, opening wide before I sped in.

Walker was standing on his porch waiting for me, and my stomach flipped at the sight of him. Keeping my eyes on the circular drive, I pulled to a stop in front of a ranch-style single-story home. It was beautiful in its simplicity. Just like his concert had been.

After I put my car in park and set the emergency brake, Walker opened my door for me and reached for my hand to help me out. I looked up at him, my eyes wide as I stood up and said, "Wow. It's beautiful." Pivoting in the driveway, I took in the gardens surrounding the house and the fountain in front of the entryway.

"Wait until you see the view." He smiled like a little boy and pulled me through the front door.

Glass windows stretched from floor to ceiling, allowing for an unobstructed view of the water and the Catalina Islands. It was breathtaking and I stopped mid-step to let it all sink in. Just yesterday morning I was fighting with my boss, certain I had killed my career, and now I was in Walker's beautiful beach home, thankful I wasn't anywhere else. When he pulled his long-sleeved shirt off, revealing a tight T-shirt underneath, I was even more thankful.

"Do you like it?" he asked, meaning the view, but in my mind I currently had two things of beauty to look at.

"It's beautiful. You're beautiful. I'd never want to leave."

He stepped behind me and wrapped his arms around me as I pressed my back against his chest. "You don't have to." Then he kissed the side of my neck, and I suppressed at shiver at the tingles his touch gave me.

Pulling away from me, he said simply, "Sit," so I made myself comfortable on the nearest sofa. "Can I get you anything to drink? Water, soda?"

"I'm okay, thanks."

The cushion next to me shifted with Walker's weight as he sat. "We haven't even talked about your job yet and what happened yesterday. I want to hear everything."

Walker's cell phone rang and he glanced down at the flashing screen before excusing himself to answer it. "I'm sorry. I need to take this."

"Of course," I responded as he pushed up from the couch and stepped out into his backyard.

I sat alone in the living room, scanning the framed pictures on his mantel and the artwork on his walls. Curious, I got up and walked over to the fireplace to inspect the framed black-and-white photos. One of Walker and his mom backstage at one of his concerts made me smile, and I fought back sudden tears. She looked so happy.

There were pictures of him with his friends, his family, other singers and musicians, and a small four-by-six photo of him and me as teenagers in the sand. I had completely forgotten his mom took our picture that summer. Walker stood holding his surfboard at his side, his other arm wrapped around my waist. I was looking up at him like there was no one in the world I loved more. And at the time, there wasn't. His head was angled down toward me as well, the smirk on his lips saying it all. He had been in love with me too. Sure, we were just kids then, but what we shared that summer had been as real as it got at the time.

"Sorry about that, but I'd been waiting for that call. It was actually about you, so..." He paused and walked in through the patio doors, a broad smile on his face.

"Me?" I drew a hand up to point at my chest in question.

He nodded and then sat back down on the couch, spreading his arms out along the back of the cushions. "I made a few phone calls yesterday to some friends. You have a couple of options, Miss Myers." His expression turned serious.

"Do I?" I narrowed my eyes as I settled down on the couch next to him, wondering what the heck he was talking about.

"As you know, I'm in the market for an agent. And I think I've found the perfect one." He stared at me, a smile spreading across his face, and I widened my eyes in surprise.

"Me?" I shot bolt upright in shock. "You want me to be your agent?" I asked incredulously.

"Yes. I will only sign with you. So you have two options. One," he lifted a finger in the air, "you can either open your own agency and I'll be your first client. Or two," he lifted a second finger, "you can go to work at the Warren Taylor Agency and

I'll still be your first client."

"Warren Taylor's? But I couldn't just go there and be an agent—" I stopped mid-sentence, my thoughts spinning too quickly for me to keep up.

Walker pressed a finger to my lips to stop me. "They said they would hire you. That I would be your first and only client until you learned the ropes and got some agency experience under your belt. They want to help you grow and they want you to learn from them. They're completely on board and more than happy to help with this transition period in both our lives. You just have to call them and accept."

He removed his finger and I smiled as big as my lips would allow. The uneasiness that had settled in my stomach over my career suddenly disappeared. "Oh my gosh, Walker, you're amazing." I crawled onto his lap, wrapping my arms around his neck. "Thank you so much. You didn't have to do that, but I really appreciate it."

He leaned his body away from me, breaking our contact. "I wanted to."

I smiled, filled with happiness. No one had ever done something like this for me before. In a town filled with people pulling strings, I never intended to play that way, and was amazed that this agency would do the same. "Do I need to call them now and work out the details?"

He tilted his head. "They can wait. I can't."

"Is that so?" I giggled against his mouth as his lips found mine, his hands gripping me tighter.

"Wait." I pulled away, forcing him to release me as I crawled off his lap and stood. "What if I'm bad at it? What if I'm a terrible agent who makes horrible business decisions?"

"You won't be. But we'll add a clause in our contract that you're not allowed to ruin my career," he said with a laugh and moved to kiss me again, my mind still racing.

I leaned away. "Wait!"

"Again?" His eyebrows shot up as a smile teased his lips.

"Last thought. I don't normally mix business with pleasure. This might not be a good idea. What if we don't last?"

"We," he said as he shook his head at me disapprovingly and rose to his feet as well, "are never breaking up. And you know it. I don't normally mix business with pleasure either, but I'm making an exception. And so will you."

Walker was right.

He was so damn right.

His hand snaked around my lower back as he pulled me toward him and our lips met. I parted my lips slightly and the tip of his tongue teased mine, tentatively at first before going all-in. Happiness swirled around me on every level, and I realized I'd never felt luckier. Or happier.

He lifted me by my ass and I wrapped my legs around his waist. "I'm taking you to the bedroom. You can thank me there."

I threw my head back and laughed. "I know I should be saying something like, 'No, Walker, this is too soon,' but we were in love once before so it doesn't count, right?"

"Doesn't count? It all counts. Every moment with you counts, Madison." He walked us through the double-door entry to his bedroom, and I gaped at the room's ocean view. I could definitely get used to this.

Walker placed me on the bed before he knelt, straddling my body with his. I reached for his arms, feeling his biceps flexing as I ran my fingers across them, tracing the tattoos that swirled down to his forearms with a light touch. His gaze trapped my own, refusing to release it as he slowly stretched out his legs, lowering his hips against mine as he rested his weight on his elbows. When I closed my eyes at the delicious tingles that began when he pressed all that wonderful male hardness against me, he said, "Open your eyes, babe. Look at me."

Without conscious thought, my eyes fluttered open as my body reacted to Walker's words and actions instinctively, no permission from me requested or needed. He asked, and I obeyed. I wrapped my arms around his neck and tilted my hips against his, trying to get closer, and closer, letting him know just how badly I wanted him inside me.

"Don't rush me." He focused on me intently, and the determination and passion I could see in his eyes took my breath away. "I plan on taking my time." A devilish smirk crept across his face and my cheeks heated.

I slid my hands over his back before grasping the hem of his shirt. Tugging on it, I forced it up until he ducked his head through the opening and discarded it onto the floor. I inhaled quickly, the sight of him shirtless even better than I could have imagined. Definitely better than I remembered. His tanned skin was beautiful, all hard and smooth at the same time, and I wanted to lick every square inch of it, especially the tattoo of five numbers in a simple, but masculine script placed above his heart.

When I traced the numbers with my fingers, I must have frowned in confusion because he glanced down at it.

"I got this tattoo once I started making money and traveling a lot. I was hardly ever home for a while there."

"What do the numbers mean?"

"It's the zip code for Malibu. I thought about getting the coordinates for our beach, but I didn't like the way it looked. Too many numbers."

I sucked in a sharp breath. "You were going to get a tattoo about me?"

He smiled. "This one's about you too."

"It is?"

"Not just you, but yeah, you're a part of it. You were always a part of my heart, even though I swear you took it with you the day you left. I wanted to carry my home with me when I was far away. My mom, Malibu, the surf, my friends, you. As long as I kept you all right above my heart, you'd always be with me, no matter where on this planet I was at the time."

My heart did a little flip-flop inside my chest. Everything this guy said to me made me feel like I was fourteen all over again, falling in love for the first time. The past few days had been straight out of the pages of a fairy tale, and I wanted to live my life in it.

"When'd you get so romantic?"

"Birth," he crooned.

Swooning a little inside, I sucked in a sharp breath, wanting that magical mouth all over me.

As if reading my mind, he tugged my shirt up a few inches, leaving part of my stomach exposed. He shifted back and dipped his head to my abdomen, touching his tongue to my skin in slow, sensuous strokes. From time to time he paused, pressing his lips to my skin, dropping small kisses here and there as he ventured to the next exposed piece of me. I gasped as he gave me a small nip, the excitement building within me almost too much to handle.

"I need this off. Now." He tugged at my shirt impatiently, then pleaded with his eyes for me to get rid of it.

"You said not to rush you," I teased, but did as he asked.

When I dropped it to the floor, his eyes gleamed with an undisguised hunger as his gaze drifted over me, dropping to my waistband before traveling back up and stopping at my breasts, encased in a skimpy satin and lace bra. Thank God I decided at the last minute to grab my sexiest lingerie; from the looks of it, Walker liked it. A lot.

He hesitated, licking his lips like I was his last meal, so I grabbed his head, my need for his mouth on mine overwhelming any rational thought. My tongue found his as I stroked it, then sucked his bottom lip between my teeth. When I bit down gently, Walker let out a moan that almost had me screaming for him to take me. How long did I have to wait until I could feel him inside me?

Fuck taking my time; I needed him like I needed air. Walker was my oxygen and I desperately needed to breathe.

"I want you," I huffed out between pants, my greedy hands pulling his hips into me, against me, onto me.

His head pulled back from mine, a half smirk on his face. "You think I don't want you? I want you so fucking bad it hurts. It's hard to go slow. It's fucking torturous," he said, dragging out the last word. "But I need to take my time with you. I want to remember every detail, every expression on your face, every sound you make. I want to make love to you like it's the last time I'll ever get to do it."

"Why would you say that?" I asked sharply, my defenses instantly up at the notion of anything ending between us.

He chuckled. "I just meant that I want to appreciate it. But if you don't let me take my time, it will be just as quick as if we'd done it when we were teenagers. And that would be embarrassing."

"Fine," I agreed reluctantly, my hormones clearly not on board the slow-moving train.

When he resumed his attention to my bare stomach, this time teasing the sensitive areas on the side of my rib cage, his tongue left a trail of warmth in its wake. I closed my eyes and threw my head back, all my senses on overload, affected by his every move. I gripped his head, threading my fingers through his short-cropped hair, my nails scratching, my fingers pulling. Wherever he was, it was never enough. I wanted him all over me, every part of him connected with a part of me. The feeling was overwhelming, all-consuming, and I'd never felt anything like it before.

After teasing every square inch of my stomach and ribs, he moved his mouth slowly up toward my breasts. With a quick one-handed flick, he unclasped my lace bra and tossed it on the floor. At least I think that's where it landed; I didn't know anything anymore. The room spun around me as Walker took the tip of one breast inside his warm mouth and began to suck. Teasingly, he switched between sucking and flicking me with his tongue as pleasure shot through my entire body. Pulling away from me, he moved to the other breast, already pebbled with desire and waiting for him.

As he gave attention to my other breast, he slid one hand down to my jeans, unbuttoning and pulling down my zipper. I tried to wriggle out of them for him, but could barely move any part of my body, I was so consumed with his mouth and the things it was doing to me.

He pulled away, all the heat from his body roughly torn away as he stood up and quickly ripped my pants from my legs. Before I could complain at the loss, Walker was back, his hot mouth meeting my skin again, but this time starting at my ankles and I hissed with pleasure. He worked his way up my calf, alternating between stroking me with his tongue, kissing me with his lips, and nipping at me with his teeth. By the time he reached my thighs, every nerve in my body was afire, and I trembled at his touch.

I moaned, arching my back as he flicked his tongue against my panties, which were already embarrassingly wet. Desperately I reached for his head, pulling and grabbing at him, wanting him to stop teasing me and get on with it, already.

His eyes burned with desire as he met my gaze before sliding my lace panties to the side and dipping his head to take a taste of me. I bit my lip to keep from releasing a pleasure-filled scream, and sucked in a breath instead.

Pausing for a second, his voice thick and raspy, he said, "I can't do this for long or I won't last, babe. I apologize in advance."

Another flick of his tongue and I was completely lost, no longer able to formulate words or thoughts. My body tensed, my entire consciousness focused with the intensity of a laser on the sensations he gave me. Little gasps and moans escaped me, and he groaned in response. He lapped at me deliberately, his tongue taking its time with each carefully placed stroke. I moaned again, my voice almost unrecognizable, and he pulled his mouth away. Part of me wanted to cry from its absence, but another part of me felt relief. We were that much closer to finally coming together the way we had always been meant to, and I had never wanted another human being so badly in my life.

The heat from his mouth was replaced by two of his fingers. They moved in and out of me as he dropped soft kisses onto my stomach, every action working in complete harmony with the other.

"You're so beautiful. I can't believe you're here. Never leave," he whispered against my skin between soft kisses.

I whimpered, the overload of sensations tearing through me, as I pushed and pulled against him, wanting to feel him everywhere, all over me at once. His hot mouth moved up my stomach, over my breasts, and landed on my neck where he delivered more achingly beautiful attention. He pulled my earlobe between his teeth as he nibbled and then sucked, his tongue sweeping around it.

My jaw line was pampered next, his mouth loving on every inch of skin it touched. His full lips pressed against my cheek before stopping just short of my waiting mouth, which I had parted in desperation for him. Walker pulled back slightly and grinned.

"You like teasing me?" I barely breathed out.

"Who wouldn't?" he said hoarsely before taking my mouth roughly, his tongue sweeping in and finding mine. Frantically, I pulled at him, digging my fingertips into his skin as I rubbed myself against him, desperate to finally feel whole.

"I need you. This has been slow enough. Get inside me, Walker. Please," I managed to get out between kisses.

"Now who's the bossy one?" He smirked, his eyes hooded and filled with want.

"I want you."

"Say it again."

"I want you. I want you inside me. Right now," I begged without shame.

He reached across me and pulled out a condom from his nightstand drawer. Impatient, the second he was done covering himself I reached for his body and pulled him back on top of me. I wanted all of him, needed to feel connected in every way to this man.

"There's no going back from here, Madison," he said as he poised himself above me. "It's you and me against the world. You understand?" His voice shook the slightest bit, much like his arms as he held himself back while holding himself up.

I nodded and he lowered his chest to mine, his expression serious. "Tell me you understand what I'm saying. Once we do this, there's no going back. We're not going to be just friends. We're not going to be just buddies, or people who work together. This is it for us."

The heaviness of his words settled into my heart and calmed it. I half expected it to do the opposite, but Walker's demands were just what I needed when it came to him. "I understand."

"Good. I couldn't take losing you twice." He lowered himself against me so that every possible part of us could touch, and the utter happiness I felt coursed through every fiber of my being.

His hardness pressed between my legs and I lifted my hips, arching my back, begging him to enter. Slowly, oh so slowly, he pushed himself inside me, and my body took him in, adjusting around him. He filled me completely and I squeezed my eyes shut, my chest tightening with anticipation as my body opened to accept more of him.

"Don't close your eyes, babe." He ran a finger feather-light down the side of my cheek, and I fought to open my eyes, when all they wanted to do was close so I could get lost in his touch.

He moved in and out of me slowly, each time filling me more fully than the last. Every pull of his body made me want to scream out to make him stop as each push back in achingly fulfilled my desires. Our bodies fit perfectly, moving together in a synchronized rhythm that built quickly, and I began to pant.

"I wanted to take this slow," Walker breathed

out against me, "but I'm having a hard time. No pun intended." Then he found my mouth again and swept his tongue swept across my bottom lip. I nibbled and sucked his bottom lip into my mouth before tilting my head to kiss his neck, to nip and lick at his skin the way he had mine. The salt on his skin turned me on even more, and I lapped at his neck greedily.

Our sweaty bodies slid against each other with each thrust, our mouths and hands desperate for each other as our passion built. My hands lowered to his ass and I pulled him harder, my nails digging into him as I pulled him hard against me.

"Walker, I think I'm going to—" I stopped short and gasped, my hips rising and pressing against him over and over again. "Oh yes, God," I cried out, louder than I'd intended as a current of pleasure ripped through me, sending shivers down my spine.

"Madison." Walker's voice shook as he breathed out my name, his eyes wild as he watched my body jerk with spasms of ecstasy. When the contractions subsided, I loosened the grip I held on his backside and moved my hands along his slick skin to stroke along the tensed muscles in his back and shoulders. He stared at me deeply, his eyes never moving from mine as tiny beads of sweat dripped down his forehead.

He began to move in earnest then, and captured my mouth with his as he plunged himself as deeply inside my body as he could. He thickened inside me as his pace quickened, each thrust finding a new depth within me. "Oh God, Madison."

I couldn't look away from him as he reached his peak, his face twisting with pleasure, his eyes closing briefly as he shuddered. His body jerked as he thrust a final time before collapsing on top of me, both of us struggling to catch our breath.

Intense happiness and contentment swept over me as I stroked his neck, his heavy weight covering me as he gasped deeply, his heart thundering against mine.

"I'll be better next time. And the next," Walker breathed out and I laughed.

"What exactly was wrong with this time, might I ask?" By my calculations, it was more than amazing.

"I didn't get to devour you the way I wanted," he said, panting for air. "But give me an hour."

He pushed up and rolled to sit on the side of the bed. I pulled up the tangled sheets around my chest and let out a happy sigh as he removed the condom, grabbed a tissue to wrap it in, and tossed it into the trash can at the side of the bed.

Crawling back into the bed, he stretched out and faced me, our foreheads nearly touching. "You realize you're never leaving this bed, right?" His hand stroked my exposed shoulder and arm as goose bumps appeared.

My heart continued to race as I came down from my Walker Rhodes high. I laughed at his silliness, and said, "I'll probably have to leave it at some point."

"Only if I let you." He raised an eyebrow and gave me a playful grin.

I poked his shoulder and teased, "I don't know who you think you are."

"The boss of you," he said half seriously. "From today until forever."

I wanted to argue just for the sake of arguing, but knew it would be futile. Walker would know I was lying. This man had bossed me around since the moment he came back into my life.

And I fucking loved it.

Eight Weeks Later...

I sat in my tiny office at the Warren Taylor Agency, filtering through my day's e-mails and waiting for my only client to arrive. The agency had wanted me to start there right away and I had obliged, beyond thankful for the opportunity. The staff and I bonded immediately over our distaste for poor business practices and even poorer bosses.

I had been wrong in my assumptions of the industry as a whole. Not everyone was a bad guy only out for one thing. So far, this company seemed to practice the ethical business standards that I held dear.

To be honest, a few of my new coworkers were wary of me in the beginning, not hiding their opinion that I only got a job because I was Walker Rhodes's girlfriend. I couldn't even   argue the notion since it was in fact, pretty true. But once they saw how hard I worked and realized that I wanted to make a decent name for myself in the business, I earned their respect and friendship.

This job had already been completely different than when I worked for Jayson. Who, speak of the devil, seemed to be just as successful as the day I left. Part of me hated him for it, but the rest of me was thankful that I didn't have to look in the mirror every day and see his face. I could hold my head high and feel good about the person I chose to be. I highly doubted that he could say the same.

"Knock, knock." Walker's voice drew my attention away from the computer screen and toward my office door.

"Hi!" I pushed back my rolling chair and ran into his arms. "I love it when you come see me in the office."

"Because seeing you at home isn't enough? You're addicted to me."

I smacked his shoulder and faked a scowl. I had practically moved in with Walker, spending nearly every night there. And I was pretty sure I'd be moving in officially before the end of the year. Keri had already approved of this plan and offered to kick me out if it would help speed up the process, but I didn't want to leave her high and dry. It wasn't like she struggled for money, but it was the principle. Besides, I liked having my own space. Not that I seemed to ever need it.

"I think you're the one who's addicted in this relationship," I told him.

"You got that right. I'm no dummy." He lifted me off the floor and planted a sweet peck on my lips.

Walker and I had fallen into a comfortable routine. Everything between us flowed easily and naturally, like we were always meant to be together.

He stopped hanging out at night clubs and I met his friends. It turned out all of them knew exactly who I was, even from before the night of the concert. Most of them had been friends with him for years, and were there through Walker's breakdown after we lost contact. They were thrilled for him, and couldn't believe we'd finally found each other after all this time.

Sometimes I still couldn't believe it either.

My parents had been just as excited when I

brought Walker home one evening. My mom had actually started crying when she saw him, saying she couldn't believe that the little fifteen-year-old boy from Malibu had turned into such a successful and handsome man. She insisted on telling embarrassing stories that Walker reveled in hearing.

I'd wanted her to stop, some of the memories were too painful to relive, but Walker had seemed genuinely interested in knowing everything I went through during our separation. My dad had just smiled, seemingly content with the chaos around him, and I felt tremendous relief at their approval. Everyone around us called our situation unbelievable, but I knew it was more along the lines of a miracle.

Walker grinned at me and set me gently back on my feet. "I'm here on official business, woman. So we should get to it."

I tugged down my black pencil skirt to straighten it and walked back toward my desk. Stalling, I fidgeted with a stack of papers as Walker made himself comfortable in my guest chair.

"Did you finish reading the script?" he asked, knowing full well that I had finished it last night.

"I did. Did you?" I countered, knowing he finished it last weekend.

"Yeah. I really liked it."

I smiled. "Me too. I think it's a brilliant first role for you. It's so different than how the public sees you, so you won't get typecast and only get scripts where you're a lonely singer or a musician on the run. I love that this character doesn't sing. Thank God there's no singing at all in the whole movie," I exclaimed, throwing my arms wide with enthusiasm.

He laughed as I recalled the multitude of scripts I'd received since the announcement in the trades proclaiming that I was his agent. Every script had included a singing role for Walker to play; it was beyond ridiculous.

That was, until the day Keri's dad had a script couriered over to me with a role for Walker that was unlike him at all in real life. It was an action flick, with Walker's character a single dad fighting for his daughter. Apparently he blew them away at the audition. I hadn't attended...by choice. Agents didn't normally accompany their clients on auditions, and I wanted to keep that line clear. Our professional relationship was already muddled enough.

"So, the contract looks pretty standard," I told him. "You're getting a really nice flat-rate paycheck with a bonus if the movie grosses a certain dollar amount upon release. There are also a couple of other bonus provisions based on DVD sales and such. Before the film is released, you have to keep quiet about the details of the story and only reveal things about your character that have been approved by the producer or director." I pushed the stack of papers toward him. "You just have to sign all the pages I've flagged."

Walker grinned and accepted the pen I offered. His hand scribbled furiously from page to page, each signature more illegible than the last. He looked up. "That's it?"

"That's it. I'll courier these back to Mr. Sampson's office, and will get in touch with your manager with regard to your schedule. They plan to film for six weeks straight, but things don't always go smoothly, so I'd plan for extra time. And then there will be a press junket afterward, both domestic and international. You shouldn't schedule another tour yet."

Walker laughed. "Another tour? I need to get in the studio and record all the new songs I've been writing first."

"Yeah, you do. You're such a slacker." I

laughed at my own joke, knowing how untrue my words were.

Walker never stopped. His head constantly churned with new melodies and lyrics. He carried a notepad in his pocket everywhere we went, and he utilized the voice record feature on his cell phone more than anyone I'd ever known—humming, beat boxing, and singing chords into it at all hours of the day and night.

And I loved it. His dedication, determination, and work ethic only made me love and respect him more.

"Well," he said. "I'll let you get back to work. I might stop by the studio on the way home and lay down some tracks. Text me before you leave to see where I am, okay?"

"Okay."

Walker leaned across my desk and gave me a soft kiss. "I love you."

"I love you too."

As he headed out of my office, I watched his backside until he suddenly stopped. He turned around, catching my gaze on his ass, and said, "Oh, Madison. I almost forgot."

I cocked my head to the side and waited.

"I got you a gift to celebrate our first movie

contract."

"A gift? Walker," I started to object, realizing I'd never get used to the way he spoiled me.

He pulled a small jewelry box from his baggy jeans pocket and my heart started to pound, completely out of control. It was way too soon for this, no matter how right it all felt. He opened the box to reveal a simple ring, a line of diamonds channeled within a solid band of platinum.

"I know it's too soon to get engaged, even though I'd marry your sweet ass tomorrow if you'd let me, Sparkles." His smile grew wider as I giggled at the nickname. "But I wanted to get you something to show you that I don't plan on going anywhere. Not today, not tomorrow, not ever."

I reached for the ring and read the words etched inside the band.

2day. 2morrow. 4ever. Walker + Madison

My eyes filled with tears as I looked up at him, my heart feeling too full for my chest. "It's beautiful. Thank you."

"Put it on. And never take it off."

When Walker slid the cool metal band onto the ring finger of my right hand, I felt a little tremor run through me. I knew without a doubt that I'd never spend another day without this man by my side.

We were good apart, but together we were unstoppable.

Thank You

I hope if you read and enjoyed this story that you know it's just the beginning. This book was meant to be an introduction into the celebrity world we all know and love (or love to hate). More stories are coming and I hope you're ready for the fun-filled ride! ᴄ

Thank you to all my readers for their support, love, and for telling me insane things like, "I'd buy your grocery list if you wrote it." I know you wouldn't really buy my grocery list, but it's funny comments like those that keep me going! I have the best readers in the world…thank you for interacting with me on Facebook and in our TPGC group. I love my Kittens!

Thank you to Pam Berehulke for her superb editing skills (and for having fun with this one!), and Michelle Warren for putting up with my constant cover changes (and then designing something more than I could have ever imagined). Thank you both for being so amazing to me. I'm blessed to have you in my corner.

And to my girlfriends a.k.a. real-life author friends…thank you for existing. Jillian Dodd, Samantha Towle, Tara Sivec, Rebecca Donovan, Kyla Linde…where would I be without you ladies to turn to? Probably on Drake's lap. LOL

And to my son, Blake, who insisted I thank him because he went to the Drake concert with me. As if sitting there in the seventh row wasn't heaven enough? LIKE HE WAS TORTURED TO BE THERE! HA! But he's right; that concert inspired this entire book. If it weren't for that night, this book probably wouldn't have happened, so thanks, Drake. You know, for existing and for being hot.

And now this just got creepy. LOL

Coming Soon

Be on the lookout for Paige Lockwood's story, coming next in THE CELEBRITY SERIES by J. Sterling.

About the Author

Jenn Sterling is a Southern California native who loves writing stories from the heart. Every story she tells has pieces of her truth in it, as well as her life experience. She has her bachelor's degree in Radio/TV/Film and has worked in the entertainment industry the majority of her life.

Jenn loves hearing from her readers and can be found online at:

Blog & Website:
www.j-sterling.com
Twitter:
www.twitter.com/RealJSterling
Facebook:
www.facebook.com/TheRealJSterling
Instagram:
@RealJennster

Also by J. Sterling

In Dreams

Chance Encounters

THE GAME SERIES:

The Perfect Game

The Game Changer

The Sweetest Game

Please join my Mailing List to get Updates on New and Upcoming Releases, Deals, Bonus Content, Personal Appearances, and Other Fun News! ☺

http://tinyurl.com/ku7grpb

Made in the USA
Lexington, KY
11 March 2014